Darcie Desires a Drover

Linda K Hubalek

Darcie Desires a Drover

Linda K. Hubalek

Butterfield Books Inc.

Lindsborg, Kansas

Darcie Desires a Drover
Brides with Grit Series, Book 7

Copyright © 2016 by Linda K. Hubalek
Published by Butterfield Books Inc.
Printed Book ISBN-13: 978-1518845994
Library of Congress Control Number: 2015918253
Printed in the United States of America.

This book is a work of fiction. Except for the history of Kansas mentioned in the book, the names, characters, places, and incidents either are the product of the author's imagination or are used fictitiously, and any resemblance to actual persons, living or dead, business establishments, events, or locales is entirely coincidental.

For order blanks for the Butterfield Books' series, please look in the back of this book, or log onto www.ButterfieldBooks.com.

Retailers, Libraries and Schools: Books are available at discount rates through Butterfield Books Inc., or your book wholesaler.

To contact the author, or the publisher *Butterfield Books Inc.* please email to staff@butterfieldbooks.com or write to PO Box 407, Lindsborg, KS 67456.

Books by Linda K. Hubalek

Brides with Grit Series

Rania Ropes a Rancher   *   Millie Marries a Marshal

Hilda Hogties a Horseman   *   Cora Captures a Cowboy

Sarah Snares a Soldier   *   Cate Corrals a Cattleman

Darcie Desires a Drover   *   Tina Tracks a Trail Boss

American Mail-Order Bride Series

Lilly- Bride of Illinois

Butter in the Well Series

Butter in the Well   *   Prairie Bloomin'

Egg Gravy   *   Looking Back

Trail of Thread Series

Trail of Thread   *   Thimble of Soil

Stitch of Courage

Planting Dreams Series

Planting Dreams   *   Cultivating Hope

Harvesting Faith

Kansas Quilter Series

Tying the Knot

Dedication

To women, past and present—

thank you for giving loving homes to children in need.

1887 map of Ellsworth County, Kansas.

PROLOGUE

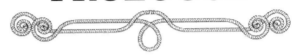

June, 1865

Rochester, New York

Reuben Shepard slowly made his way up four steps to stand on the porch of the brick house. The War Between the States was finally settled and Reuben had spent weeks getting home from Georgia, catching rides with whoever would give him one, walking the rest of the way. His body was very thin and malnourished, thanks to the horrific conditions of the Confederate prison camp where he spent almost a year. He may look like an old, sick man instead of a young man in his prime at age twenty–eight, but at least he made it home alive. Over a third of the prisoners in the Andersonville Prison died from disease, hunger or fights in the overcrowded place. Reuben drew in a breath of clean air where he stood, relishing the air wasn't full of humidity, stench and rotten food anymore. *I'm finally home!*

Reuben lifted his hand to raise the knocker on the front door to announce his arrival. He didn't want to shock his wife and son by walking into the house unannounced in his condition. They'd think he was a beggar breaking into the house to scrounge for food.

He listened as steps made their way from the foyer to the front door. Reuben held his breath, so anxious to see his family again.

But instead of Mattie, a tall man, probably in his mid–thirties opened the door. Reuben stared at him, at a loss of what to say. He held a baby girl against his chest with one arm.

"Father, who is that scary man?" A young boy popped his head underneath the man's arm to stare at him. Then a little girl moved around the man, wrapping their little arms around his knees and stared at Reuben.

Confused, Reuben asked, "Does…Mattie Shepard still live here?"

The man hesitated before he gave a quick nod, but he stayed in the doorway preventing Reuben from entering the house.

"Matilda? Could you come to the foyer for a minute please?" he said over his shoulder, never taking his eye from Reuben.

Reuben tried in vain to peer around the man to see his wife. He wanted to see her, hold her, and tell her how much he'd missed her all these years.

Mattie came to the door, looking over the arm the man still had across the door frame. He may have looked like a ragged, dirty scarecrow, but after a few seconds Mattie recognized him. Her blue eyes grew wide and she put her hand over her mouth while she sucked in her breath.

But before Reuben could get over the shock of seeing her, she shook her head instead of pushing aside the man's arm to get to Reuben. Mattie drew a deep breath, placed her hand to rest on the man's arm, and plainly stated, "If you're looking for my *first* husband, he was killed early in the War. *This* is my husband, Reginald Ringwald and *our* three children. Shut the door, Reginald, I don't want the children catching a disease from the filthy beggar."

Then the man shut the door in his face, while he stood there with his mouth open, staring at the brass knocker.

"What? *What did you say?!*" Panic raced through his heart as her statement rolled through his mind. *Mattie had said I was dead, and she'd remarried? Three children…it had to be his son Gabriel, and the little girl looked to be around four years of age.*

He was killed early in the war... and must have been declared dead almost immediately for Mattie to have a daughter that old. Was the girl *his child*, too, instead of...what was his name, Ringwald's?

Adrenaline pumped through his body as Reuben repeatedly pounded on the door. He waited for someone to open the door, but no one did. Reuben pounded again, then tried to open the door. It was locked.

He put his hands around his face as he peered into the window on the porch but saw no one. Reuben wobbled around the side of the house to get to the back door and found it, too, was locked. Pounding on it didn't get any results there either.

Reuben wandered the backyard for a while, taking in the change of the shrubs and flowers and the swing *he* didn't put up in the oak tree. *I'll sit on the porch a bit, surely Mattie will come out to talk to me.*

Hours passed before he finally left his house, hoping he could find food and shelter somewhere, because his wife had turned him away.

The next morning, after sleeping in an alley and scrounging in a barrel behind a restaurant for food scraps, Reuben went to the courthouse. There, Reuben found the record of his "death" two months after he'd enlisted. He also found record that Reginald Ringwald bought his way out of military duty and married the "widow" Matilda Shepard four months after his "death".

Reuben walked out of the courthouse and walked south out of town. There was no use trying to connect with any of his other family members now. Besides being legally dead, Reuben really did feel like he was dead to the world, and decided to leave it that way.

Darcie Desires a Drover

CHAPTER 1

Eight years later, August, 1873

Rochester, New York

Reuben stood on the porch of the Rochester home where he, his wife and son had lived before he enlisted in the war. Not much had changed in the neighborhood. The two–story brick house sat on a quiet street, lined with mature trees. Wrought–iron fences surrounded each neatly trimmed lawn in the block of houses. The marigolds in the front window sill flower boxes were starting to wane as the summer came quicker in New York than Kansas.

He hesitated to knock, not because he didn't want to see Gabe, but because there was a black ribbon wreath on the door, showing an adult had died in the house not long ago. A white wreath would have meant a child's death, and a mixed wreath of black and white ribbons would have signified an older child's death. So was it Reginald, Mattie or possibly one of their aged parents living with them who had died?

After taking a deep breath, Reuben firmly knocked on the front door. It was time to connect with his son again.

"The door crept open and an older lady, dressed in a maid's uniform questioned Reuben, "May I help you, sir?"

"Yes, ma'am, I'm here to see Mrs. Ringwald. Is she available?" Reuben held his breath, hoping the woman wouldn't tearfully reply the mistress of the house had died.

"May I ask your business with Mrs. Ringwald? She just lost her husband earlier this week." The woman's mouth was pursed, probably wondering why a man in western clothes was standing on the rich widow's porch.

"I'm an old acquaintance of the family wanting to give her my condolence, ma'am. I'm from out of state, visiting family nearby and I heard the news," Reuben sighed in relief knowing it wasn't Mattie who had died; but this visit may be harder because of Ringwald's death.

Reuben wondered if there was a black wreath on the front door for him when he "died". Mattie certainly hadn't worn black mourning clothes for a year before she remarried, according to the courthouse records he'd seen eight years ago.

"Very well, if you'd wait in the parlor, I'll let Mrs. Ringwald know that Mr....what was your name, sir?"

"No need to tell her. She'll see me," Reuben said, while stepping forward so the woman would move out of his way. He turned to the left, knowing exactly where the parlor was in his former house.

Besides the change in curtains, the parlor room looked the same. Memories bounced through his head as he looked around the room. The settee where he and Mattie had cuddled and kissed many evenings was still in the same spot. So was the overstuffed chair he sat in, holding Gabriel the first months of his life, watching his tiny rosebud mouth pucker a few times before finally falling asleep. Reuben remembered both he and Mattie sitting on the floor, Gabriel walking his very first steps from her arms to his, and feeling the sense of overwhelming pride of what his little man had just accomplished.

Reuben walked to the fireplace mantel to study the framed portraits of Mattie's family carefully lined up on the top of the stone surface. Mattie and her husband. Mattie and her daughters when they were infants. Mattie's parents. His son was in a family portrait taken probably a year or so ago, but only one daughter was in the photo. Apparently they had lost their youngest daughter sometime in the past eight years.

Of course, Gabriel's baby picture wasn't up here, because it would have shown Reuben proudly holding Gabriel sitting in the studio chair, with Mattie standing beside him with her hand on his shoulder.

It was the summer of 1859 when Miss Mattie Vanderwig took a fancy to him while he had been driving a carriage for hire in the area. She came up with reasons to hire Reuben and they spent the summer conversing, with him in the front seat and Mattie chatting away in the seat behind him. Before Reuben knew it, he was smitten with her attention…and her plan. She dressed him up, presented him to her family and announced they were getting married, never mind that Reuben hadn't asked her father's permission for them to marry. Her family had lots of money and Reuben thought he was set for life.

He and Mattie moved into this house, owned and furnished by her parents. Reuben was shocked by the balance in Mattie's new bank account for their living expenses, but it was in her name only. Looking back as a mature adult now, rather than a young man of twenty–one, he knew her parents intended to control the money.

But, at the time, Reuben was excited to be chosen by the beautiful girl, not realizing Mattie had chosen him to rebel against her parents. Instead of making a living driving a carriage, he spent his days wishing he had something to do, besides occasionally ride a horse, or take Mattie to dinner parties.

But the birth of Gabe changed everything and made the marriage worthwhile. He had a son to carry on his name. And because he didn't have to work, he spent the next two years doting on his son.

Then southern states started to secede from the Union and formed the Confederacy. When the Confederates attacked Fort Sumter in South Carolina in April of '61, it was news in the paper, but not something they thought would last long, or affect them in New York.

Everyone thought it would take a month or so to end the war and get the Union back together. Reuben was caught up in the excitement of traveling down the eastern coast to help finish the war that fall. He wouldn't be gone long enough for Gabe to miss him.

But instead, Reuben was forced to fight four long years of battles—states away from home—worrying whether he'd still be alive at the end of the day, swallow any halfway decent food to satisfy his constant hunger, worrying whether his family was safe in New York.

And all that time, Mattie was living with another man.

After not being permitted to reunite with his wife and son after the Civil War, Reuben had wandered out of New York, going from job to job until he ended up in Kansas. Then Reuben signed on as a chuck wagon cook and saw a lot of country between Kansas and Montana as cowboys drove livestock to the new ranches starting up in the West. He'd become proficient working with cattle and horses over the years and enjoyed the physical work, the challenges of the weather, the simpler life.

For the last two years he'd stayed in one place, at the Bar E Ranch near Clear Creek, Kansas. His main job was taking care of the bunkhouse and the young ranch hands who watched the longhorn cattle roaming over the six thousand–acre ranch. He cooked, cleaned, performed first aid and gave advice to the ranch hands, who were barely out of their teenage years. Reuben was only thirty–six, but he secretly enjoyed the boys thinking he was wise in his old age. He also drove the chuck wagon and cooked along the trail when his employer sold and delivered cattle to other ranches.

The Bar E owners, Cora and Dagmar Hamner, were good employers and Reuben was satisfied with calling the place his permanent home.

Or he had been, until Darcie Robbins, Millie Wilerson's sister from Chicago, came out to help at the ranch house when Cora's family, the Elisons, traveled from Boston to Kansas for Cora's wedding.

14

Darcie and her two children, a toddler, Tate, and a baby, Amelia, were living in the ranch house now. Much to Darcie's chagrin, her two–year old boy had immediately taken to Reuben, wanting to be with him constantly. And Tate's attention made Reuben's heart ache for the two–year old boy he last held before the War.

Reuben knew it would be hard to go back East to see his family, but it was time. He was older and wiser, believing his family would want to know he was alive after all. Reuben asked for a month off to travel to New York, and Darcie would take care of the cooking and cleaning of the bunkhouse while he was gone.

His first order of business was to see if his parents or siblings still lived in the area. It turned out Reuben's two brothers, Lowell and Elton, actually did die during the War, and his parents had passed on since then, as well. But, he was reunited with his two sisters, Betty and Louise, and their families, catching up on the last dozen years.

"Mother, I want my letter from the lawyer!"

"Hush, Gabriel, Flossy said we have a guest in the parlor. He'll hear you!" Reuben heard Mattie say as mother and son walked down the hallway toward the parlor.

Reuben turned to the double door entrance of the room, waiting for the first glance of his son. Would Gabriel's hair still be dark brown like his, or have changed to match his mother's lighter–brown hair?

"The letter was addressed to me personally, and the lawyer said it was about my real father. I have a right to know who he was and where he's buried!"

Reuben stared at the teenager walking sideways into the room as he continued to argue with his mother. He was as tall as his mother now, but skinny and pale, like he'd never physically worked or been outside a day in his life. Mattie was dressed in an expensive black silk gown, fitting for the widow of rich man.

Reuben turned his attention to Mattie when she said, "We'll talk about this later, Gabriel."

"Why don't we talk about it now, Mattie?" Reuben challenged her. He watched as she gave him a baffling look, and then gave the same to Gabriel.

"Excuse me, sir, but what did you just say?" Mattie said, not recognizing Reuben.

"I said, why don't we tell Gabriel his father's name—*is, not was*—Reuben Shepard, and that I'm very much alive..."

Eleven days later, Clear Creek, Kansas

Reuben Shepard glanced over at Gabe again. It had been a long trip from Rochester, New York to Clear Creek, Kansas. As each day passed of their week–long train ride heading west to the frontier, the boy looked more out of place in his fancy white shirt, suit coat, trousers and polished leather shoes. Not that his clothes were clean now, and the same could be said of Reuben's clothes. Reuben rubbed a hand through his dark brown hair, staring at the boy sitting on the bench facing him as he did so, seeing the same color hair, his stormy gray eyes, his face starting to change the way teenagers do, along with his squawky voice.

Gabe and his mother exchanged terrible accusations after Reuben made his surprise appearance at their house. His son was upset because he thought Reginald was his father until the lawyer announced "and to my *stepson*, Gabriel, I leave a letter about your real father." Why hadn't they told Gabe about him? Why no one had ever slipped and told Gabe before now was a surprise.

The final blow was Mattie screaming that now Reuben was here, he was in charge of his son because she didn't want to see him again. The maid helped them pack Gabe's things in a trunk and a carriage was conveniently parked out front of the house to get them off of Mattie's property. Another staff member must have taken Gabe's sister, Mary, out the back door while they were packing, so Gabe didn't get a chance to speak with her before they left. Reuben returned the next day to see if Mattie had calmed down and changed her mind, but she had refused to see him. Reuben had no choice but to take Gabe home with him.

Mattie refused to give Gabe his letter from the lawyer, too, even though it was addressed from Mr. Ringwald directly to Gabe. Reuben had the driver stop at the lawyer's office to ask about the contents of the letter. But the man was away for a period of time, so Reuben left a note explaining the situation, and asked the lawyer to contact Reuben in Kansas when the lawyer returned to his office.

Reuben sighed and rubbed a hand over his forehead now, wishing he could rub away the tension headache that had been plaguing him since he left Rochester.

He and his son were complete strangers, neither of them was comfortable being with the other, so conversation was still stilted between them.

"Why aren't there any houses out here, except a few now and then?" Gabe asked as he rested his head against the window glass, staring at the endless prairie.

Considering Gabe hadn't talked much so far, Reuben thought he'd better try to get a conversation going. So far the boy's talk had been about being hungry, then griping about the sandwiches they'd been buying at the little towns along the way. Reuben had only so much money along for this trip, and hadn't planned for it to cover the cost of a second train ticket and food for two people.

"Before the war, there wasn't anything but herds of buffalo and tribes of roaming Indians living out here on the open prairie. Then the government started giving away free land in Kansas and the railroad was built across the state. Only then did people travel out here to homestead the land and build houses and towns."

"Why would anybody want to live out here? It's so dirty and hot," Gabe scrunched up his nose as a gust of hot air blew in the top half of the open car window behind them.

"Yes, summers are hotter here than New York, but you get used to it. Weather varies all over the United States. When I was in Georgia..." Reuben stopped, not wanting to mention that time.

"When were you in Georgia?" Gabe showed some interest, but Reuben hated he had brought it up now.

"The last year of the war," was all Reuben could say.

"Were you in Andersonville? We read about it in school and…I've seen some pictures of the soldiers there."

Reuben nodded, not wanting to think about those horrible conditions.

"Is that why you didn't come home…to us?" Gabe gruffly asked.

Reuben stared at his son and couldn't fathom what was going on in the boy's head since all the lies of the past years erupted in Mattie's parlor over a week ago.

"I *did* come back to you, but your mother had remarried, said I had no claim on you, my home…" Reuben tried to keep the bitterness out of his voice, but by the look on Gabe's face, he wasn't succeeding.

But now his son was with him, and Reuben had to rebuild their relationship after being years apart. The trouble was: his son's life had been turned upside down with his step–father's death and leaving his home, and Reuben didn't know how to be a parent to his sad and sullen teenage son.

Reuben put his elbows on his knees and rubbed his hands over his face. Maybe he should have stayed dead instead of trying connect with his son again. Would Gabe have been better off if he hadn't gone to New York?

CHAPTER 2

"Take off your boots by the door and walk easy. I don't want the angel food cake to deflate," Darcie called back to whoever was stomping into the bunkhouse. The ranch hands had been so good lately about helping her keep the bunkhouse clean, and now someone was tromping in dirt on the clean floor.

"Reubie!" Darcie's two–year–old son Tate squealed in delight and charged across the room to the door of the bunkhouse.

Darcie drew in a deep breath before she turned around, knowing Reuben was standing in the doorway. Reuben had traveled to New York last month to visit family, and now he was back.

She glanced back to see Tate charging toward the door where Reuben Shepard stood with a carpet bag in hand. Reuben looked tired in rumpled travel clothes, but he gave his attention to Darcie's son as he always did. Then Reuben looked around the room and locked eyes with her, causing Darcie's breath to catch in her lungs.

Darcie had mixed feelings about seeing Reuben now. For one thing, she'd be losing her current job, now that Reuben was back to take over the care of the ranch hands and bunkhouse. Luckily, Cora had asked Darcie to stay and help in the main house, because Cora was with child and having a terrible time with morning sickness. Darcie didn't know how long Cora would need her to stay, but Darcie hoped it would be a long time. She liked the ranch and the people who lived and worked on the Bar E.

And second, Darcie was attracted to the man, although she and Reuben seemed to ruffle each other's feathers now and then, so to speak. Her ex–husband dealt out pain through physical violence and words causing her to mistrust men. But she always felt safe with Reuben, and all the men in the extended family which had pulled her little family into theirs.

"Hello Reuben, welcome…" Darcie stopped mid–sentence as she realized not only was Reuben staring at her, but also a young man with similar features.

Tate interrupted the adults by plowing into Reuben's knees. Reuben set his carpet bag on the floor and picked up her son. "Hey, Tater Man, how's my favorite little cowboy?" Tate patted Reuben's cheeks before wrapping his chubby arms around Reuben's neck. He laid his head on Reuben's shoulder for a second before pulling back and looking Reuben in the eyes. "Missed you," Tate said while cocking his head to one side.

"Who that?" Tate went on to say, pointing to the unhappy–looking teenager standing next to Reuben.

Reuben paused a second, then cleared his throat. "Darcie, and Tate, I'd like you to meet my son, Gabriel." Reuben awkwardly gestured for the young man to move up beside him. The boy was the spitting image of Reuben.

"I go by Gabe, not Gabriel," Reuben's son said in an unhappy voice.

The scowl on the boy's face deepened as he stared back at Reuben, then around the room before settling back on Tate. Reuben inhaled a breath but it didn't sound strong enough to give him any strength. "He's fourteen, and he's going to be staying with me for a while. His stepfather died recently and his mother decided it would be best if he spent some time with me."

"No, she kicked me out when you showed up," Gabriel grumbled before glancing at Darcie then back at Tate.

Darcie was caught off guard. Reuben had never mentioned he had a son, and this old? Why hadn't he ever said anything about the boy to her?

She wiped her hands on her apron and walked forward to shake Gabe's hand. "Welcome to Kansas, Gabe," but the boy ignored her outreached hand until Reuben roughly nudged him in his side.

"Remember your manners," Reuben said with a low growl. Apparently the two had been getting on each other's nerves during their trip here.

Darcie rubbed her hand down the side of her apron when Gabe didn't take her hand. "That's all right, Reuben, I…"

"No, it is not. He has to learn to respect others, especially his elders," Reuben shot a glance at his son again.

"Sorry," Gabe mumbled, but he didn't sound very sorry about it.

"Well, please take off your boots and put your things in your room. I'll have coffee and some cookies ready for you in a little bit. I'm sure you're hungry," Darcie tried to defuse the tension between the two.

"Why would I take off my boots?" Reuben's eyes narrowed at Darcie.

"Put there," Tate pointed to the row of boots against the side of the wall.

The bunkhouse door opened before Darcie had time to answer Reuben's question.

"Welcome back, Reuben," Eli Fisher, the ranch foreman, happily said while toeing off his boots and setting the pair against the wall. "If we'd known you were coming into town today, we could have picked you up," Eli reached out to shake Reuben's hand, then offered it to Gabe. "This must be your son, Gabriel. Welcome, young man."

Eli knew about Reuben's son, *but she didn't*? "Sit down, Eli, I was just ready to get the afternoon coffee on the table."

Reuben stared around the room, finally looking at the things she'd changed in the bunkhouse after he'd left.

"What in the...horse apples have you done to my bunkhouse?!" Reuben's face tightened up as he met her eyes.

"Isn't it great?" Eli said as he looked around the room, too. "The men really like the new look of their home. We haven't had one cowboy quit since Darcie spiffed up the place. I want her to decorate my foreman's cabin next," Eli went on, not noticing Reuben was drilling a hole in Eli's head with his stare, as the foreman smiled at Darcie.

"After I washed the windows, inside and out, I noticed it could use...a woman's touch to make the men feel at home here."

"It's a bunkhouse, not a parlor with a grand piano in it. And what's with the 'take off the shoes' comment?"

"You take off your boots at the door, then there isn't dirt, mud and manure to clean off the floor. So I suggest you do it, before you go into your room, Reuben and Gabe," Darcie pointedly said, while Tate pointed at the floor again, too. Even her little boy had learned the rule and took off his boots when he came in the door, most of the time.

Darcie and her children stayed in the cook's quarters in the main house, but spent most of their time in the bunkhouse. Dagmar furnished the bunkhouse with two high chairs and a crib which she used when the children needed to eat or nap during the day. It had been a perfect set up for the three of them. How would their arrangement change now that Reuben was back, with a son in tow to boot?

"You whitewashed the walls, and added red–checked *curtains*?!" Reuben's hands were on his hips, looking at the combination room of living area and kitchen. Reuben lived in the separate living quarters on the end of the house.

"Did you do anything to my room?" Reuben's eyebrow was cocked and his eyes were ready to fire darts at Darcie.

"Yes, it was my top priority," Darcie said smugly, "I shoveled out the dirt before I added *pink* curtains to the two windows."

22

For some reason, she never felt like cowering when Reuben talked to her, compared to her husband anyway. But then she had learned to stand up for herself and get had regained some of her self–esteem since her days with Curtis, too.

"I tell you, the hands have turned civilized, if that's possible with a bunch of young bucks," Eli continued. "They take their dishes over to the dry sink after meals, say please and thanks, and take turns reading to the children in the evenings before Darcie takes them back over to the house."

"Were they all heathens before Darcie took over?" Reuben wanted to know.

"No, but they just act better because there is a woman and children in here with them during the meals. Toby and Del are too far away from home to visit their folks, so it's helped with their homesickness and their work."

"So am I out of a job since it's been taken over by Darcie, *who does everything so well*?" Reuben stared at Eli awaiting his answer.

"Reuben, you're being rude in front of…" Darcie started to talk before the door opened again.

"Hey, Reuben! Glad you're home!" Dagmar Hamner's booming voice startled Gabe as the ranch owner entered, having to duck his head to enter the bunkhouse. Although the Bar E Ranch deed listed his wife's name, Cora made it clear to everyone she and Dagmar were partners, so he was considered an owner, too, by the hands.

"Thanks, Swede. I'd like you to meet my son, Gabe," Reuben nodded his head to Gabe while shaking Dagmar's hand.

"Nice to meet you, Gabe. I'm Dagmar Hamner. Ready to ride the range for the brand?" Gabe was hesitant; he did shake Dagmar's hand, but cringed like his hand had been squeezed too hard. Being a half foot over six feet tall, with long, disheveled blond hair, Dagmar was intimidating to people until they got to know him. And his thick Swedish accent was a little hard to understand at times.

"Not sure I still had a job here when I walked in to find *Darcie* had taken over the bunkhouse." Reuben's eyes slid from Dagmar's to Darcie's and back to their boss.

"I figured you'd work your way back to Kansas after your visit north, so Darcie was just filling in for you," Dagmar stated to Reuben before gesturing to Darcie. "Actually, Darcie is going to stay and cook and clean for us in the big house, now that my wife can't stand the smell of cooking bacon and eggs."

"Why, she sick?" Reuben asked in concern.

"Nope, happy as a brooding hen, but morning sickness has knocked her off her horse for a while," Dagmar smiled broadly, waiting for Reuben to figure out his hints.

"Congratulations, Dagmar," Reuben responded. "There's nothing more exciting and frightening than holding your firstborn in your arms the first time..."

Reuben took a quick glance over at Gabe, but didn't say more. Reuben had to have been in his son's life at first, so what happened to cause their separation?

"But before you take over the bunkhouse again, you'll be a drover. Next week we'll drive a herd of mixed cattle to a ranch east of Fort Hays."

"How many head?"

"About four hundred, a mixture of cattle from us and the Cross C. Isaac and Cate are going along, so Cate had planned to drive the chuck wagon and fix our meals. Then, instead of coming back with us, they're boarding the train to visit Cate's sister in California—as sort of a late honeymoon," Dagmar answered.

"They finally got married? Well, I'll be..."

"Oh you missed a lot of drama while you've been gone. Sarah Wilerson left Ethan Paulson at the altar and took off after Marcus Brenner on Nutcracker, Hilda's race horse, before he left to go back to Fort Wallace. Turns out they never left the Cross C Ranch because Widow Sullivan delivered triplets, with Sarah's help.

"So did Sarah and Marcus marry while I was gone, too?"

"Married and adopted the widow's six children because she passed in childbirth. Plus Marcus went back to Fort Wallace to identify two children who had been living with the Cherokees, and brought them home to add to the family."

"Cookies," Tate tapped Reuben's shoulder since Reuben was still holding the tot. Tate was anxious for his afternoon treat.

"Why don't you men sit down to drink your coffee while you visit? Tate is getting anxious for his cookie, then it's nap time for him."

The three men sat down around the big room's table, immersed in their conversation, ignoring Gabe who still stood by the doorway. Darcie walked toward him, motioning to Reuben's carpet bag still sitting on the floor. "If you'll take the bags, I'll show you to your room, then you can come back out for milk and cookies." Darcie counted to six before the boy did as she asked. "Follow me, please," and she turned to lead the way, assuming he'd eventually follow.

It wasn't very many steps to get to the other side of the room, but the boy took his time. Reuben's room was partitioned off the end of the bunkhouse by a wall for some privacy. It had the luxury of a door and a small pot–bellied stove to keep the room warm during the winter months.

"Why am I staying here?" Gabe asked with disgust.

"Well, I figured you'd stay with your father. He can pull in a cot for you or you can sleep in one of the hands' beds when they're out overnight watching the herd."

"Why stay here with the help, when the house is available?"

Darcie stopped to wonder what Reuben had told his son about the Bar E. "The ranch owners, Dagmar and Cora Hamner live in the house. I, and my children also live there, in the help's quarters off the kitchen."

"I'm not staying in this crude room."

"Well, you'll have to bring that up with your father. I'm not in charge of the living arrangements." Darcie turned and walked out of the room. She knew Tate would be a handful during his teenage years, but hopefully he wouldn't be as rude and ungrateful as this young man.

Reuben rose from his chair when he heard Darcie walk back into the room. "I'm sorry, I keep forgetting he's with me. I should have shown him to my room."

"He wasn't happy to see it, but he did flop down on your bed when I was closing the door."

"Gabe's tired, upset...and his step–father recently died," Reuben said, after sitting back down and running his hand back and forth across his forehead.

"Oh, dear. No wonder he's acting out of sorts," Darcie said, thinking of the poor boy's actions now.

Reuben looked up at Darcie, before looking down at his cup of coffee. "I've never said anything about my past life to you, because I didn't think it was anything I could change." Everyone stayed quiet, waiting for Reuben to talk again if he wanted to say more.

"I went home after the war ended, found out I had been declared dead, and my wife had remarried. So I left and never went back."

Darcie couldn't imagine the heartache that must have caused Reuben.

"But then being around Tate reminded me of my son, who was Tate's age when I enlisted. After all these years of pushing back the bitter hurt, I felt drawn to finally go back home to see what happened to him and my family."

Now she understood the man a little better. All this time Reuben was suffering from his loss, and now he'd faced it, finding more problems apparently.

"Is Gabe's mother still living?" Eli asked. Darcie hadn't thought about the fact that Gabe could be an orphan now.

"Yes. Mattie, and her twelve–year–old daughter, Mary, still live in the same house we lived in when she and I married. Mattie had a second daughter, Eleanor, but she died before she was two years old. I saw the toddler when I was there in '65, but Gabe says he doesn't remember much about her.

"When her husband's will was read, it revealed Gabe was his stepson. Gabe didn't know that the man who raised him wasn't his real father until that moment. His step–father left a letter for Gabriel, supposedly to reveal my name, but Mattie took it and hid it somewhere. When I arrived, Gabe and Mattie were arguing about the letter because she wouldn't give it to him. Then Mattie blew up and told Gabe to get out of the house.

"I don't know how this will work out between us, or if he'll want to go back home, and if she'll let him. We're strangers, but this is our chance to be together for a while."

"It will work out, Reuben. He's got space and freedom to think about his family. And we can put him to work to keep his mind occupied, at least part of the time," Dagmar assured Reuben.

"But that's going to be a problem, because I'm sure he's never had to work for a thing in his life." Reuben hung his weary head. "I hate that he's not going to earn his keep here."

"Again, give it time. Now you take the rest of the day off to get rested up yourself. I see you used a horse and buggy from the livery stable. Eli, have Peter take it back to town."

Reuben nodded, drained his cup of coffee, and rose out of his seat. "I appreciate that. Except for cat naps on the train, I haven't slept for days."

Reuben's yawn and dark circles under his eyes showed the stress he was under. Darcie couldn't imagine not seeing Tate again until a dozen years later. They'd be strangers, too.

"Where Reubie going?" Tate said while tugging on her apron.

"You're going to have to be patient, Tate. He's tired and needs a nap, like it's time for you to do." Darcie picked up her son and carried him over to the crib in the corner of the room. Seven–month–old Amelia was already asleep, curled up in an innocent pose, oblivious to the conversation at the table not far from her. "Lay by your Sissie and be quiet for a while," Darcie whispered in his ear when he started to protest. She laid him in the crib and rubbed his back for a few minutes until his breathing evened out.

She couldn't help hearing the raised voices in Reuben's room. Darcie hated to admit it, but she felt sorry for the gruff man. His marriage had shattered when his wife declared him dead and wed another. Those acts by the heartless woman would affect Reuben and his son forever.

It was satisfying seeing her son, Tate, running with glee after the ranch dogs. Tate's nap was over too soon and he was outside with her as she hung wet sheets on the clothes line. The two–year old would never catch Yipper and Kipper unless the dogs wanted him to catch them. And, occasionally, one of the dogs would plop down waiting for the toddler to tumble on top of it. Darcie never knew if the dogs got tired running around or got tired of watching Tate run around. Either way, the animals were always gentle with Tate.

Darcie turned her attention to the wet sheets blowing in the late summer breeze. She could probably take them down again in a few minutes because they'd be dry soon. She couldn't get over the difference in smell and cleanliness between sheets and clothing washed and dried here compared to Chicago or St. Louis where she'd lived in the past. Items dried in the prairie wind brought the smell of sunshine, if it could be labeled. Clothes dried in the cities always smelled like polluted air, or the trash the clothes lines hung over in the alleys between the crowded buildings in the Chicago area where she grew up.

Everything in Kansas made her breathe easier, after living through the abuse her husband Curtis had delivered to her and Tate. At first it was just verbal abuse, diminishing her self–esteem. Visits from her father, Ennis Donovan, and a fellow Chicago policeman to Curtis, and her sister Millie had kept Curtis from doing physical violence to her. But the abuse turned violent after Curtis left his job with the Chicago police force. He moved them to St. Louis without allowing her to let her family know where they were going to stop them from intervening.

Thanks to her new dear neighbor, Flora Davis, Darcie was able to send letters to her sister. Millie arrived in time to help Darcie deliver her baby Amelia, then left Darcie in Flora's care. Millie had answered a mail–order bride advertisement and needed to travel to Kansas to meet her groom. Millie took Tate with her, then Darcie eventually followed with her baby, and her father, who had followed Millie to St. Louis.

Darcie could have gone back to Chicago after her husband was in jail for the murder of a fellow officer, but Darcie liked being with Millie and her husband's extended family. Kansas may be considered the uncivilized western frontier by Chicagoans, but Darcie felt safer here, and liked the cowboys, who were strong male role models for Tate

Would she ever marry again, at least to give her children a father? She should, so they'd have a permanent home and provider. Darcie had stayed with her sister for a month, then worked at the Cross C Ranch a while before coming here. Her children were happy, but Darcie felt like her life continued to take one step forward, away from Curtis, and then stalled again.

"Mrs. Darcie, Sweet Pea's awake and done pooped a smelly pile in her diaper," Peter Young, one of the cowboys walked toward Darcie, holding Amelia at arms' length. The baby had been sleeping in the bunkhouse in a crib in the kitchen. Hard to tell if she woke up by herself or was nudged into waking up by Peter or one of the other hands. They loved to make a fuss about her, until it was time to change her diaper.

"Peter, you probably scraped more manure off your boot to walk into the bunkhouse than she has in her tiny diaper. I've showed you all how to change her. Why don't you do it instead of bringing her out here?" Darcie shook her head, but knew it was because Amelia was a baby *girl*, more than the smell of the diaper.

The hands didn't mind cleaning up Tate if he pooped in his drawers by accident. Of course, that usually meant taking Tate outside, stripping him down and washing off his backside at the outside pump with a rag.

"When you get married and have babies, Peter, you'll need to be able to handle dirty diapers, whether it's on a boy or girl," Darcie reminded him before taking Amelia into her arms.

"Oh, I suppose," Peter answered as his cheeks turned red. Why hadn't Curtis been like the men around here?

"I'm going to miss Tater and Sweet Pea when you aren't working in the bunkhouse, Mrs. Darcie. They sure liven up the place," Peter scraped his foot back and forth in the dirt. "What will you do when Cora's back to snuff again and can take care of her own house?"

"I'm not sure yet," Darcie answered, not wanting to uproot her children again so soon, but maybe it would push her to find what they all needed, a permanent home. Unfortunately, she may have to marry again to do so, but it would only be with a kind and reliable man this time.

CHAPTER 3

Reuben went to church when he wasn't required to be on the ranch, usually sitting with the Hamners and Wilersons in their two, well now three pews, after meeting all of Sarah's new brood. Today he sat with a fidgeting Gabe on one side and Dagmar on the other. Cora sat next to Dagmar, with Darcie and her kids on the other side of her. Darcie usually sat with Millie and Adam, but their pew was already full by the time the Bar E group arrived at church.

Reuben had worried Gabe hadn't packed any church clothes, but soon realized that's all the boy had along, by Clear Creek standards. They had made a trip to the general store to outfit him for living on the ranch. But so far, the new clothes were clean, unfortunately.

Deep in thought, he was startled when Tate crawled into his lap. He leaned forward to look at Darcie who shook her head and motioned he needed to send Tate back her way. As long as the toddler was quiet, Reuben would let Tate sit with him, so he ignored Darcie's command. Tate sat sideways, leaned onto Reuben's chest, and started sucking hard on his thumb while staring at Gabe. Reuben put his arm around Tate so he wouldn't tumble off his lap by accident. He looked down in time to see Tate give Gabe a defiant grin, pulling out his thumb long enough to stick his tongue out at him.

Reuben couldn't help smiling to himself, realizing Tate was jealous of Gabe. And the way Gabe made a face back at Tate, made

Reuben think of the rivalries and fights he and his brothers used to have. Gabe had to be missing his sister, but he hadn't said a word about her yet. Reuben didn't look forward to when that dam of emotion broke loose for Gabe. Reuben couldn't feel anything but animosity toward Mattie right now, so how was he going to show sympathy for what Gabe must be feeling for the loss of his family?

Everyone was standing for the last hymn. Tate put his arms around Reuben's neck, not about to let go when Reuben stood. The toddler's action felt good and sad at the same time. His son used to do the same thing as Tate, but now they were strangers to one another. Would they ever get back to the closeness they had a dozen years ago?

"This is my son, Gabriel. He's visiting from New York," Reuben was trying to keep introductions simple when people asked as they stood around outside after church. The tension in his stiff neck was about to pop a blood vessel. The questions were embarrassing to both him and Gabe and he wished he could spare his son the inquisition. Most people at church were really caring but there were a few nosy old bags with their self-righteous attitudes to contend with.

"Why didn't we know you were married and had a child?" Reuben wanted to tell the inquisitive women it wasn't their business to know.

"Why isn't your wife here with you?" Because she's still in our home, mourning the death of her second husband.

Now Gabe stuck to his side like glue, ignoring everyone's stares. Reuben glanced the direction Gabe was looking and realized he was watching Pastor Reagan's boys as they stood to the side of the congregation, probably cracking jokes about Gabe's fancy clothes and shoes.

"I'll look forward to having Gabriel in school next month," Miss Bonner stated, eyeing Gabe like he was a fresh cut of meat. The spinster teacher, on the downside of forty, had always considered Reuben fair game in the matrimony game in town. She was probably calculating how to use Gabe to snare Reuben as her future husband, which would *never* happen, Reuben was confident to believe. He'd learned his lesson about women's schemes to marry with Mattie.

Neither he nor Mattie had thought about Gabe's schooling during the heat of their argument. A lot of boys in frontier towns were finished with their education by Gabe's age and working. If Gabe was in Rochester, he'd continue learning until completing his education in a college. It wasn't a wonder Gabe looked around town in distaste and confusion. He was used to going to church in a stone cathedral, and a multi–story school house, not simple wooden structures made by local town folk working together to build what was needed in their community.

"What grade will you be in this fall, Gabriel?" Miss Bonner changed her attention to Gabe since Reuben was ignoring her. He half listened to Gabe answer the many questions she was firing at the teen, all the while searching to find where Darcie was standing. Tate was still clinging to his chest, not worrying about his momma at all, so why was *he* looking for her then?

What if Gabe was with him permanently? Should they move to town so Gabe could continue his education? What would Reuben do for a job? He didn't have enough money to buy a house, but he could rent rooms at the boarding house, he supposed. Darcie's and Millie's father, Ennis Donovan and his new wife, Flora, had moved from Chicago to Kansas to be near his daughters, and had bought the town's boarding house to live in and run as their business.

Being a retired policeman, Ennis would be a good influence on Gabe. Flora would be a grandmotherly type to dote on Gabe, besides taking care of their meals and washing.

Reuben would see Darcie, Tate, and Amelia now and then when they were in town to visit, unless the Bar E wouldn't need a new ranch cook and Darcie moved back to Clear Creek, maybe even to her father's boarding house. Hmm, then he'd get to see the woman every day.

Or, maybe he should find a wife to take care of Gabe. Not that there were a lot of available candidates in the area when men outnumbered women, probably five to one in the county. He could place an advertisement in a matrimony newspaper, hoping to get a nice woman like Millie, Darcie's sister. Reuben had been alone so long he didn't relish the idea of living with a woman again though.

Kaitlyn Reagan and her six sons headed toward them. Reuben stepped back, letting Mrs. Reagan introduce her sons to Gabe, because he wouldn't get a word in edgewise anyway when this exuberant woman took over. But that was all right because it would be good for Reuben to make some friends.

"How are you surviving the inquisition?" Marshal Adam Wilerson asked out of the side of his mouth while standing behind Reuben.

"Ready to shoot off my mouth to these busybodies, but I guess that's better than drawing my gun. You come over to save me from the next wave of questions?"

"No, you're on your own with this gaggle of females lining up to ask you such important questions. Do you realize you look like husband material standing here holding Tate, with another child next to you?"

Whoa, he didn't want to look like an easy target to these women. "Tate, I think your Uncle Adam wants to hold you now," Reuben said as he started to pry Tate's arms off his neck, which caused the boy to scream in his ear. Did Gabe act like this when he was two–years old?

"Sweet Poo–tater, want to go see our cat and doggie? They missed you when you moved out of our house," Adam sweetly bribed Tate to move into his arms.

"You realize Tate has you wrapped around his finger, not giving in to you until he gets what he wants?" accused Reuben.

"Bet you did the same thing with Gabe at this age, if you think about it," Adam countered.

"Probably. It just seems like it didn't happen, when I think about it. Now he's almost grown and I don't know him."

"You've only been together a short while, so give it time. I came over here to invite you and Gabe to have Sunday dinner with us," Adam continued.

"I don't know. I thought about eating at Clancy's." Why was he hesitating, when he knew Millie's cooking was much better fare than the café's?

"Why? Gabe needs to get to know people, and you two sitting across the table at the café staring at each other ain't the way to do it."

"True. Darcie and the kids eating with you?"

"Of course and Cora and Dagmar, too. Since you all came into town in the same wagon, guess you don't have much choice, huh?" Adam pointed out, while holding a giggling Tate by his chubby little arms and swinging the boy sideways, close to the ground, back and forth between the two men.

"Reuben," Mrs. Reagan called to get his attention, "Gabe will be eating dinner with us today and then the boys in town are getting together to play baseball. Can you come back into town around three o'clock to fetch him or should Angus or Fergus drive him back to the ranch?"

Startled by her question, Reuben looked to Gabe to gauge his reaction. Did he really want to spend the afternoon with the rowdy Reagan bunch?

"Which would you prefer, Gabe?" Reuben asked to let him make up his own mind.

Gabe looked up at Reuben, then down before answering, "Uh, will you still be in town?"

"Yes, I'll be over at the marshal's house for dinner, so you can meet me there when you're done with the game," Reuben offered, because he guessed Gabe wasn't so sure about being left in town by himself.

"Sounds like a good plan," Mrs. Reagan happily responded while winking at Reuben. "Come along, Gabe." She wrapped an arm around Gabe's shoulder and pulled him toward the parsonage.

"Guess you're off parent duty this afternoon," Adam said, before lifting Tate up to his hip. "Unless you want this little rascal back," he amended as they started walking toward Adam's and Millie's home.

Reuben looked back at Gabe walking away, then over to Tate squirming on his uncle's hip. Children needed parents, no matter their age. Maybe he should seriously think about getting a wife.

"You know," Adam said nonchalantly as they walked the three blocks between the church and Adam's house," Gabe needs a mother, and Tate and Amelia need a father."

"Gee, what are you trying to hint at, Adam?" Reuben sarcastically asked.

"I know, I know. You may think it's not a good idea to marry Darcie because you're at odds with each other half the time, but those sparks flying between the two of you... could make a good and interesting marriage."

Reuben watched Millie and Darcie, who were walking about five yards ahead of them. Amelia was on Darcie's shoulder, looking back at them, while chewing on the lace collar of her mother's dress. She was such a sweet baby with her little downy swirl of bright reddish–orange hair on top of her head. Darcie's hair was a tad bit darker red than her children's. Tate's bright carrot-colored hair was going to cause some fist fights in the future for the boy. It was a perfect match to his Grandfather Donovan's hair, though, so the older man could give Tate tips on how to handle future problems. Maybe that's why the Irish immigrant had been a prize fighter when he first arrived in America.

Reuben remembered Gabe at both Amelia's and Tate's ages and the awe of watching a little human developing in body and personality. Did he want to raise children who weren't his flesh and blood, like Darcie's children? Did he want more children in his future? That could go along with marrying again.

Sparks did tend to fly between him and Darcie, and maybe it would make life interesting...if he wanted to get married again. But right now, he had enough on his plate to figure out how to be a parent to Gabe.

"How are things going between you and your son?" Millie asked as she passed the mashed potatoes over to Reuben.

"Oh, I think, *not good* covers it," he replied curtly. "He won't talk, so it's hard to get to know him."

"He's far away from home, possibly for the first time in his life, mourning the loss of his step–father, and stuck with a stranger. I'd say he has a right to be sullen and sad for a while," Adam added.

"What are you doing to meet him more than half way?" Millie added.

"Tried getting him to work with me, but he's clueless about ranch work. We don't have anything in common except the first two years of his life, which, when I refer to, he walks away," Reuben spoke sharply, frustrated at his son's behavior and everyone asking about it, even if they meant to be helpful. But it was making him feel worthless that he couldn't reach his son.

"Are you taking Gabe along on the cattle drive, or leaving him at the ranch?" Millie questioned, probably to keep the conversation going.

"No, he'll stay in the big house with Cora and Darcie. He hasn't been here long enough to learn how to ride a horse, let alone herd cattle. I'm scared to death he'd get hurt."

Millie got up from the table, picked up the empty gravy bowl and went into the kitchen. After transferring more gravy from her skillet on the stove, she brought the refilled bowl back to the dining room table.

"I enjoy every meal of yours, dear wife. I thank the Lord every day—and twice on Sunday—you answered a mail–order bride advertisement to come to Kansas," Adam dramatically said while placing a hand over his heart.

Everyone chuckled at his statement, but Reuben knew what they went through before they were married. It was a trial taking care of Tate, who came with Millie, and worrying where Darcie was at the time, but the couple came out stronger because of it.

Reuben noticed Darcie hadn't joined in on the conversation. Tate, sitting in a high chair the Wilersons kept for his visits, was quietly playing and stuffing peas in his mouth, so she wasn't having to concentrate on her son. Amelia was napping on a pile of blankets on the living room floor. Darcie wasn't eating, but staring out into space, lost in her thoughts, apparently.

Everyone welcomed Millie's sister and her children, but he sensed she felt a burden having no home of her own. Plus her former husband's past abuse and crimes made some people think less of her, even though she was the victim. She looked older than he knew she was, but at least she'd gained weight since arriving in Clear Creek. She had been a walking skeleton, with a tiny, underweight infant in her arms then. Thank goodness her father had found them and brought them here to be reunited with Tate and Millie.

"Darcie. Darcie, you aren't eating today. You feel alright?" Millie asked.

"Fine, I'm…just thinking about what to fix for the ranch hands' meals while Reuben is gone for a few days."

"I'm sure they'll be enjoying your sweet rolls and cream pies again. Reuben never makes anything fancier than biscuits," Dagmar complimented Darcie, while winking at Reuben.

Darcie gave Dagmar a faint smile, then turned her attention to Tate. What was she thinking about today? It was hard to tell with women. He had thought he had known his wife, but Mattie had changed husbands without a hint of remorse.

Reuben watched as Darcie glanced around the table, seeming to stop as she looked at the couples seated around them. He and Darcie were the only single adults here, surrounded by couples with good marriages. Darcie had a wistful look on her face, as though she wished she could be a part of a couple, too.

How would Darcie handle a second marriage if asked? Someone could help raise her children, just like Ringwald had raised Gabe.

Reuben thought of Curtis Robbins, Darcie's husband; when he arrived in Clear Creek this past summer after tracking down Millie. Robbins demanded Tate be handed over to him, and Millie be put in jail for taking Tate to Kansas. Every man around the table, including him, stood between the aggressor and those he threatened. It still made Reuben's blood boil thinking of how the man had treated his wife and child.

How could you tell your children their father was an abuser and a murderer? Would it be better that they didn't know? It made Reuben think of Gabe not knowing about him. Ringwald stepped up and took over his job of raising his son. Did he and Mattie think it was better that Gabe didn't know about him? Probably, so to keep their secrets buried about what they had done to get together.

"Reuben?" Adam said his name and Reuben realized everyone around the table was staring at him.

"Sorry, what was the question?" He had been so absorbed in thinking about the woman across the table that he wasn't paying attention. Reuben had better start paying attention, or this family of schemers would have him and Darcie married before he finished this meal.

"Why don't you go check on Gabe, and take Tate and Darcie with you. I'm sure Tate would like to see the boys playing ball," Adam suggested with a slight smirk on his face.

So, was that an innocent suggestion, or one to throw him and Darcie together? And which did he wish it to be?

Darcie Desires a Drover

Chapter 4

Darcie looked out the kitchen window, watching the current round of disagreement between Reuben and Gabe, which they were having in the middle of the ranch yard. She glanced back at Cora, who was sitting at the table eating her late morning snack of toast and tea.

"They're at it again." Darcie didn't need to tell Cora who because they had witnessed it several times this week. Cora came to stand beside Darcie. They couldn't hear the actual words, just far–off raised voices.

"Teenagers are hard enough to raise, let alone one with a rage of hurt inside," Darcie felt sorry for both of them.

"Oh, my brothers were a handful without any major stress in their lives. And their teenage rebellion years lasted well into their twenties as you well know from stories you heard at our wedding. Poppa was at his wit's end when he sent Carl and Lyle out to the Bar E Ranch, but I'm glad he did, so I could move out here," Cora smiled at Darcie.

"Wonder what they are fighting about this time," Darcie murmured. Gabe would yell something, then walk away. The Reuben would answer, following after him. Then the two would reverse directions as they continued stomping and raising fists in front of everyone who could see them from the barn and house. They acted like two bulls challenging each other in the pasture. Darcie snickered, thinking how much they acted alike even though they hadn't been together for the past dozen years.

"Chores, school, horses…take your pick or choose a new topic. Reuben tries too hard, then blows up when Gabe doesn't do as Reuben tells him to do." Cora shrugged her shoulders, apparently not as worried about it as Darcie was.

"I hate they aren't getting along. Reuben has missed his son so much, and now they butt heads about everything." Darcie wished there was a way for her to help, but so far, Reuben bristled if anyone offered advice.

"Dagmar told Peter to take over Gabe's riding lessons, because Reuben was expecting too much too soon from Gabe. I don't think Reuben adds in the factor that being around horses can be daunting, let alone sitting high atop one."

"Peter's close to Gabe's age and pretty easygoing, so I think they'll become friends—if Gabe can get over the idea that the working class is way below him."

"We can't fix Gabe's problems in a few days, so everyone has to be patient," Cora said as she turned away from the window.

Darcie continued to stare out the window. It was a hot morning and both males' shirts were wet with sweat. Reuben's back and arm muscles bulged from all the work he had done. Gabe was a young, slender version of his father. Reuben was a little shorter in stature than most men, so Gabe would match Reuben's height in his next growth spurt. Darcie wondered how tall the men were in Mattie's family because Gabe could be several inches taller than Reuben by the time he reached maturity.

Curtis was average height, slender and wiry, because he spent a lot of time walking on patrol. He had a thin face, with a lock of light brown hair that was forever falling down on his forehead. At first, she loved to brush it back, but after they were married, Curtis slapped her hand away when she tried it. She thought she had known Curtis so well, but he was a totally different person when their courting ended with their marriage.

But watching Reuben, she instinctively knew he'd never raise a hand against Gabe. Probably because she'd learned firsthand the signs of an abuser. Darcie continued to say a prayer daily, of thanks that Curtis would never hurt her and the children again.

Now Reuben had his arm across Gabe's shoulder and they were headed for the back porch. Halfway there, Reuben looked up and caught her watching them. Darcie stepped away from the window, embarrassed she had been caught.

"They're heading for the house. I think I'll see if they want a cinnamon roll," Darcie said excusing herself and walking out the back door to meet them.

Gabe warily eyed Darcie, but Reuben looked like he was relieved to see her. "I just pulled a batch of cinnamon rolls from the oven, so I thought I'd ask if you'd like one or two. She held the screen open for Gabe to walk into the kitchen, then Reuben let Darcie enter next. He always automatically did simple gestures like that, while Curtis had expected Darcie to do it for him instead.

"Thank you, Darcie. I believe we've worked up an appetite for your rolls this morning. We could smell them before we even got to the house, couldn't we, Gabe?" Reuben responded, trying to work his son into the conversation.

"Yes, sir," Gabe quietly replied, then stepped back to the porch to wash up in the basin left on a side table for that purpose.

Darcie stepped over to Reuben and put a hand on his forearm as a silent message of comfort to him. He put his hand on top of hers and gave it a gentle squeeze to thank her. Their relationship had changed over the past week since Gabe moved in, and she enjoyed the new closeness it had brought between them.

"What have you been doing this morning, Gabe?" Cora asked as she sat back down to her plate of toast. She'd be ravenous for a cinnamon roll this afternoon, but for now she stuck with toast.

"Went through the harnesses, bridles and saddles," he shrugged his shoulders while answering.

"They need to be in good repair for our next cattle drive, and Gabe did a good job of inspecting and cleaning them. We repaired worn leather now, so we wouldn't have problems with them on the trail." Reuben praised Gabe. *So what was the argument outside?*

"Can I take another roll and go back to the bunkhouse to eat it?" Gabe asked, but didn't look up at any of them when asking.

"Sure, and take one pan of them with you for the rest of the hands," Darcie pointed to the two pans of rolls cooling on the side table. Gabe mumbled a thanks before pushing through the screen door.

Reuben sighed and rubbed his hand across his face once Gabe was gone. "Want a cup of coffee with your roll, Reuben?" Darcie wanted to ask what happened out in the yard between him and Gabe, but decided it wasn't her business so she quelled her curiosity.

"He wants to go back to Rochester," Reuben blurted out. "How can you tell a child he can't because he doesn't have a home there anymore?"

Cora and Darcie looked at each other, now knowing what they were fighting about outside. Should they give him advice, or just let him ruminate about it aloud?

"Haven't had a word from Mattie asking him to come home. I fully expected a telegram to be waiting for us when we got to Kansas saying 'send Gabe home now'. Sounds like he's not close to his grandparents, which doesn't surprise me since he's *my* son instead of Ringwald's."

Reuben stared into space while he took a sip of coffee, then bit into the roll. After one bite, he put the roll back on the plate, like he didn't have an appetite for it now.

"And he's angry at the man who he thought was his father, but now he's gone, so he can't confront him."

"So Gabe's angry at you instead, Reuben. He's hanging on to that emotion instead of giving in to his grief. Be patient with him, that's all you can do for now," Cora responded. "I see Dagmar riding in from the pasture, so I'm going out to talk to him."

"I wish Tate wasn't napping. I need a hug from the little guy," Reuben confessed after taking another sip of coffee.

"And I prefer he sleeps another thirty minutes so he's not cranky later on." Darcie wished she could wrap her arms around Reuben to give him a hug since Tate wasn't available. What would Reuben think of that? And why was she thinking of doing it?

***

"*Nooo!* Gabe go, Poppa Reubie stay!" Tate screamed while fighting to get out of Darcie's arms as Reuben prepared to mount his horse.

Poppa Reubie? Darcie looked down at her son as he squirmed in her arms, then met Reuben's shocked eyes.

"*Stay home!*" Tate yelled again while tears ran down his chubby cheeks.

"Tate, Reuben will be gone for a little while, but he will be back," she tried to sooth him.

Reuben handed Dagmar the reins of his horse and walked back to Tate's outstretched arms.

"Hey, Tate," Reuben let the little boy grab his neck, so Darcie released her hold on Tate. Not so much because of her son, but because Reuben was standing so close to her she could smell his shaving powder, mixed in with a little horse and leather.

"We're driving cattle to a buyer so we'll be gone for a few days. But I'll be back before you know it," Reuben softly said to Tate, who had buried his tear–streaked face in the crook of Reuben's neck.

"Gabe go. Poppa Reubie stay," Tate said between sobs.

"I'm sorry, Reuben. He hears Marcus' children call him Poppa Marcus, so that must be where he picked up calling you Poppa," Darcie tried to explain Tate's reasoning.

Was that a look of regret or longing on Reuben's face when she tried to explain away Tate's name for him.

"I guess that makes sense."

"Tate was upset for over a week when you left for New York," Cora added. "He looked everywhere for you, the poor tyke."

Darcie could feel the blush bloom on her face when Reuben looked at her with questioning eyes. How did she respond to that? She shrugged her shoulders and said, "He missed you."

"Yeah, I'll have to confess I missed him, too," Reuben said softly while looking over Tate's head to Darcie.

Reuben gently peeled Tate's arms off his neck so he could look at the child when he spoke to him. "I'm sorry, Tate, but I do have a job to do, so I have to be gone for a while."

"You be back?"

"Yes, I promise, son," Reuben patted Tate's back to comfort him.

"I want Baker's Kiss!" Tate demanded.

"Tate, that's enough. You don't have a boo–boo we need to kiss to make better. Plus, we don't have the tins of magic sugar and cookies out here, and we're not going to go get them now either," Darcie said reaching to take Tate out of Reuben's arms. "But you and Gabe can have some cookies when we go back into the house," she said as a bribe to get Tate to go into the house.

Tate patted his tear–stained cheek while looking at Reuben. They all knew what Tate wanted, so Reuben gave Tate's cheek a loving kiss. Darcie's sister, Millie, started the "Baker's Kiss game" while Tate was with her and Adam before Darcie arrived in Kansas.

Millie had formed small round shortbread cookies, and pinched up a bit of dough on top before she baked them to give a little handle for her to dip into the tin of fine sugar. Millie ground sugar with a mortar and pestle to make it very fine and added a little corn starch to make the sugar stick better to the skin.

Millie would take the special cookie, dip it in the special sugar, and pat Tate's boo–boo. Then she'd wet her lips and carefully touched her puckered mouth on his skin, taking off a bit of sugar, leaving the imprint of a kiss on his arm. The simple act made Tate feel better, plus he got to eat the little cookie afterwards. Now Darcie kept tins of sugar and cookies for his little hurts in their room, too.

"Feel better now, Tate?" Reuben asked.

"Umm maybe," he grunted while still pouting. "Momma needs Baker's Kiss."

"Tate, those kisses are for children, not adults."

"Nuh uh. Unca Adam kiss Auntie Millie," Tate argued back.

Okay. She knew Tate would argue forever, or scream his head off, so Darcie tipped her face up to Reuben, hoping he'd take the hint and give her a quick kiss on her cheek to satisfy Tate.

After a second, Reuben leaned down, but kissed her lips instead! She stared at him in shock for his bold move, then blushed, realizing she liked his kiss.

Tate whispered something in Reuben's ear which made his face turn beet red, but Darcie didn't hear what he said.

Darcie automatically wrapped her arms around Tate when Reuben thrust him out to her.

"Thanks for taking care of Gabe while I'm gone, Cora. I'm sure he'll feel more comfortable in the big house than he has in the bunkhouse," was all Reuben said before walking away to take the reins back from Dagmar and mounting his horse.

Darcie followed Cora up to the house to watch the herd leave from the porch. Eli, with Gabe at his side, opened the corral gate and stood back to get out of the cattle's way. Dagmar gave a sharp whistle and Yipper and Kipper ran into the corral along the inside of the fence to get around the cattle and push them out through the open gate. Isaac rode in front of the herd as the leader, Peter and Zach, on horseback on either side of the gate, waited until the herd was out, then rode up on either side of the herd to ride flank. Dagmar and Reuben rode drag behind the cattle herd and the extra horses, which were along for switching rides. Cate drove the chuck wagon's horse team behind the herd.

"I wish I was going along on this trip," Cora sighed, juggling Amelia on her hip so she could wave when Dagmar turned back to look toward the house. "Dagmar and I have never been apart since I moved to Kansas."

"They'll be back soon," Darcie said to assure Cora.

"I know, but I'll miss my giant Swede. Of course, Hilda argued with Dagmar that their mother was on a cattle drive each time while with child with the four of them and got along fine. And so I should be able to ride along, too."

"So why didn't you go?"

"Dagmar would have been too worried about me and our first baby. I think the fresh air would have been good for my morning sickness, but he would have been trying to take care of me instead of the herd. After we have a handful of kids, he'll expect us all to help with cattle drives like his family did while he was growing up," Cora chuckled.

"I look forward to meeting their mother when his parents return to Kansas. I'm wondering if she'll be outspoken and wild like her daughter, Hilda, or quiet and reserved like Hilda's twin Rania," Darcie mused.

"From Dagmar's tales, Annalina Hamner is a little of both. It will be interesting to see what she thinks of me, a former Boston socialite, as her daughter–in–law," Cora laughed.

"Want down," Tate squirmed trying to get out of Darcie's grasp. "Want cookies," he looked up at her with a pout on his face.

"Dagmar's parents will enjoy having you in the Hamner family," Darcie said as she looked back at the herd moving west.

"And I think the Shepard family, meaning Reuben and Gabe, would enjoy adding you to their family, too, seeing the kiss Reuben gave you a few minutes ago," Cora said with a teasing smile.

"It was for Tate's benefit, not mine."

"Would you like it to mean something between the two of you?" Cora's voice turned serious.

"I'm not sure I'm ready to marry again. I should, for my children's welfare, but Curtis still haunts my thoughts at the oddest times," Darcie squeezed her eyes shut thinking of the abuse the man had dealt her and Tate.

"Most men are *not* like your former husband. Do you think Reuben is interested in you?"

"I'm not sure. Reuben is scarred from his marriage, and the war, too. I don't know if he could ever let someone into his heart and life again," Darcie replied, as she looked at her friend.

"Don't give up on him if you'd like to pursue a marriage to him. I think Tate already has the two of you paired up in his mind."

Tate looked up and studied her and Cora, catching on they were talking about him. "Then I think it's time to distract T–A–T–E with *you know what*," Darcie announced while lowering Tate to the porch floor and opening the screen door for Tate to run into the house.

***

Reuben had looked back as the men left the ranch. Specifically, to the porch where Darcie and Cora stood, watching them move the herd away from the corrals. Darcie still held Tate, but he didn't seem to be bawling or causing a fuss as they left.

Tate calling him Poppa Reuben still shocked him hours later. He was gone for a month on his trip to New York, but the kid latched back onto him as soon as Reuben was back on the ranch. It was flattering the toddler looked up to him, but it made things tough between him and his own son. Tate wanted him to be his daddy, and Gabe did not, simple as that.

Reuben's face heated up thinking of what Tate whispered in his ear before Reuben handed him back to Darcie. *You kiss momma, you married.* I suppose he got at impression living with Adam and Millie, and all the other couples he'd seen kiss in church at their marriage ceremony.

He'd meant to kiss Darcie on her cheek, but her pretty face turned up at him made his lips zero in on her mouth instead. It had been so long since he'd kissed a woman, it's a wonder he remembered how.

His impulse reminded him of kissing Mattie when Gabe was Tate's age. A dozen years changed so many lives. What if the war hadn't disrupted their lives? Would he have gotten restless from doing nothing but living off his in–laws' wealth?

No. Reuben was committed to Mattie and his son, and he would have done anything to take care of his family. Why hadn't Mattie believed in his love and vows?

Looking back now, he was fairly certain Ringwald had courted Mattie before she picked Reuben for her groom. Apparently she had regretted doing so, and found the war a convenient way to switch husbands. Reuben guessed Mattie never did love him, just used him as a pawn.

At least now that Reuben had seen Gabe, he knew Mattie and Ringwald didn't get together until after Reuben left for the battlefields. Mattie and Ringwald were similar in hair color and eyes, but Gabe's facial features exactly matched Reuben's dark features. It was like looking in the mirror, twenty years ago, since he and his son looked so much alike.

Time had faded Reuben's broken heart over his shattered marriage. Instead of being bitter at Mattie, he should be glad she had some years with the man who she truly loved, but he wasn't. Ironic that Rueben, though "dead" lived longer than Ringwald. He snickered at that recollection.

Reuben thought of Darcie and the little bit he'd heard about her marriage. Why would a man hurt his wife and child? Curtis Robbins took a vow before *God* to love and protect his bride forever. Reuben could tell the mental damage Darcie's husband inflicted on her still plagued her at times when he saw her involuntarily cringe around a certain type of man.

Would she remarry again if asked? Probably, for her children's welfare if she trusted the man who asked. Apparently

Tate, in his two–year–old mind, thought he and Darcie were married now because of the kiss the boy had conned him into giving her.

He had to admit it, the simple kiss stirred some feelings in his heart that had been dormant for a long time.

"Hey, Reuben, the beans smell like you're burning them. Got something else on your mind besides cooking our supper?" Zach asked as he walked up beside Reuben. "Maybe thinking about a certain woman and toddler we left behind this morning?"

Cate had traded places back a while; she was riding his mount and he was driving the wagon team. Reuben had driven the chuck wagon ahead and around the herd to set up camp by a creek where they had stopped on a previous cattle drive. His mind had wandered while he fixed their meal, so Zach asked a legitimate question.

"Thinking about my son," Reuben answered, not wanting to say what he'd really been daydreaming about. He leaned over to stir the pot though, because he smelled the beans scorching, too.

Cate walked up while taking off her riding gloves. "Need any help with the meal, Reuben?"

"Thanks but I'm fine, Cate. I'm sure you'd like to walk around to get the kinks out of your legs," Reuben replied, as he continued to stir.

"I must admit I'm feeling a bit bow-legged. Lately I've been chasing grandchildren on foot instead of wayward cows on horseback." Cate's face was covered with dust and her shirtwaist soaked with sweat, but she still looked happy. Marrying Isaac and helping with Sarah's adopted family had given Cate a new purpose in life.

"We'll be doing neither in a few days when we get on the train for our honeymoon," Isaac reminded her, taking off his hat and hitting it against his thigh to knock off the dust. Isaac and Cate were boarding the train at Russell to travel to California to visit Cate's sister. Their trunk was in the chuck wagon, ready to be dropped off at the train depot. Their horses would travel back to the ranch with the drovers and wagon after delivering the herd to the buyer.

"It was nice to meet your son in church last Sunday," Cate continued the conversation after sitting on the wagon tongue and stretching out her legs in front of her. "Did you plan to bring him back to Kansas with you?"

"No, but my showing up for a visit was his mother's excuse to pawn him off on me. Unfortunately I don't know what I'm doing, except I need to make up for the twelve years I wasn't in his life," Reuben said shaking his head.

"Give yourselves time to get to know each other. Be genuine and ask about his life at home, what was his favorite class in school last year. Ask about his friends, what he did for fun," Cate gave Reuben her advice.

"If you start with easy topics, the hard stories will come out eventually. Has he talked about his family?"

"Just a comment or two until he realizes it and clams up again," Reuben answered while filling a plate of beans and bacon for Cate.

"Want a corn pone, too?"

"Please. I'm hungry enough, I could eat two," Cate sighed as she stood up to take the tin plate from Reuben. "I'm so glad you thought of bringing some folding camp stools along. I don't think I could get back up off the ground in my current shape."

He and Isaac chuckled at Cate's remark because they were tired and sore, too, and they weren't done with their day yet. Dagmar, Zach and Peter were quietly walking their horses around the herd to settle them down for the night. Reuben, Isaac and Cate would take a turn in a few hours so the other three could eat and rest.

"And another part of Gabe's problem is Tate, whether he wants to admit it or not. I'm sure it hurts Gabe that Tate and me are close. He didn't get to have the connection Tate and I have built, almost as father and son."

"Then it's natural for Gabe to compare Tate as a sibling, whether it is in a good way or bad. When Sarah was born, my sons were at odds on how to deal with a baby. Adam, at age six, thought she should get up right away in the morning to help with chores. Five–year–old Jacob tried to play with Sarah like she was a puppy, and Noah was four and mad about being displaced as the baby of the family. But they'd do anything for each other back then, and still would now as adults."

"You know, I don't know how close Gabe and his sister are, since he hasn't mentioned her much yet. The old fairy tale *Cinderella* came to mind when I helped Gabe pack for his trip. Not that he was forced to be a servant, but I bet Mattie, like the bad stepmother in Cinderella's story, favored her child with Ringwald over Gabe.

"I'm sure Gabe never had to worry about monetary needs, but Ringwald never adopted him, even though I was supposedly dead."

"That's got to give the boy a chip on his shoulder, whether he knows what it is or not," Isaac shook his head while giving his observation.

"Yes, unfortunately. Gabe has the bad attitude of a rich boy who deserves everything money can buy, yet he's lonely because money didn't buy him love from his own family," Reuben continued.

"So he's a confused young man now, stuck in a place that is very foreign to him, Reuben," Cate said, pointing a finger at him to stress the point. "But this is your opportunity to show him how to be a good man, because he's only a few years away from being on his own."

"Yeah, and I don't feel qualified to do that," Reuben hated to admit out loud.

"Then this is your opportunity to let other people help you both out. Get him involved in school and church," Isaac suggested.

"Our ranching families blend together so much that Isaac and I are 'Grandpa and Grandma' to all of them, even though we're not related to any of them. We'll naturally give Gabe the structure of family I think he craves. In fact, Gabe is going to spend a few days in town with our family while you're gone."

"And I bet I'm the last to hear about this, aren't I, Cate?" Reuben worked hard not to growl at the woman.

"Didn't Darcie mention it to you?" Cate asked, as if she was surprised.

Isaac shook his head at his wife. "Apparently not since Reuben didn't know about it. What did 'Saints' Catherine and Flora and their committee plan for Gabe"? Isaac arched his eyebrows at Cate, challenging her to confess their strategy.

Reuben inwardly groaned. Cate and Flora Davis Donovan, nicknamed "The Saints", helped Millie and Darcie through their difficult situation when Millie was hiding Tate from Darcie's abusive husband.

"Ennis and Flora have an empty room in their boarding house so Gabe will stay in town with them next week. That way he can, for example, play ball with other kids his own age, help 'Aunt Millie' deliver pies to the hotel, or walk with 'Uncle Adam' when he does his early evening check around Clear Creek."

"Cate, I can see the little ones call Adam and Millie their uncle and aunt, but Gabe's a little old for that, don't you think?" Reuben asked.

"No, not when Ennis and Flora become Gabe's grandparents, too," Cate said with a straight face.

"What? No, Darcie's parents are Tate and Amelia's grandparents, not..." Reuben looked at Cate, who still looked innocent, but next to her Isaac was trying his hardest not to burst out laughing.

"So you two and your ladies' committee, who I'm sure is involved, have planned for me to ask for Darcie's hand in marriage, so the five of us can become a 'happy family'?"

"What? We never thought of such a thing...but that's a brilliant idea. If you can wait for a short time, we'd love to be at your wedding. Isaac and I should be back in about three weeks, so plan the wedding a month from last Sunday."

When had the women gotten together and planned his future? He and Gabe only arrived ten days ago. Poor Gabe, alone in town, with a band of good but scheming women. Well, he'd either love Clear Creek by the time Reuben arrived back to the ranch, or would have hopped on a train to New York already.

And Cate's remarks would make him think about Darcie every day he was away from her—and the simple "Baker's Kiss" they'd shared.

CHAPTER 5

"Gabe, why'd you change into your Sunday clothes to eat supper?" Jim Gibson asked as Gabe joined them at the dining room table in the ranch house.

Gabe moved into an upstairs bedroom this morning when Cora suggested it instead of staying in the bunkhouse without his father. Darcie was sure it was more similar to what he was accustomed, and they could keep a better eye on him.

"Jim, back East, proper gentlemen dress for dinner, instead of just splashing water on their face to look half-way presentable at the evening meal," Cora tried to ease Gabe's mind, because he had assumed he had to change for the evening. Gabe's face had turned red with embarrassment at Jim's question. "You might consider at least changing your shirt, too, Jim, before coming for suppers in the house."

Eli and two other ranch hands, Jim and Ker Lundgren, joined them for the meal so Darcie didn't have to cook two separate meals. All three of them glanced down at the fronts of their shirts to see how clean their clothes were.

She had fixed a typical evening meal with vegetables from the ranch garden, canned meat from last winter's butchering, homemade rolls and an apple pie for dessert.

The men passed the serving dishes to get their plates full of food and commenced to eat wholeheartedly. Darcie was glad to see

Gabe noticed their hunger for food and followed suit. She knew he hadn't eaten much the first week in the bunkhouse, so maybe he'd start now if around people other than his father.

"Beans!" Tate yelled while hitting his spoon on the front tray of his high chair to get some attention.

"Tate, you need to say 'Please pass the beans'," Darcie corrected him, while Cora, on the other side of Tate, put a little dollop of mashed potatoes on the toddler's plate as that bowl came around.

"Gabe didn't," Tate stuck his chin out in protest.

"That's because Gabe politely waited until the bowl was passed to him," Darcie patiently said. It was surprising how jealous Tate was of Gabe, but then he'd acted the same way when he had to get used to his baby sister.

"Gabe, I think Tate is a little jealous of you," Cora observed. "I assume you and your sister tease and fight every now and then, too?"

Gabe didn't reply either way.

"You haven't said much about your sister, Gabe. How old is Mary?" Darcie inquired.

"She's twelve." Gabe laid his fork on his plate, looking like he just lost is appetite. Darcie guessed he was missing his family. "I...didn't get to say good–bye to her before I left," Gabe quietly added.

Everyone was quiet when Gabe made his last statement. Why didn't he get to talk to his sister before he left with Reuben?

"I still sorely miss my brothers and sisters at times," Ker said as he stared intently at Gabe. "I left Sweden about your age, and haven't seen my family for ten years now."

Gabe stared at Ker as his words sunk in. "Why did you leave?"

"Too many of us in our family and not enough food. I had to strike out on my own so my parents could feed the younger children," Ker shrugged his shoulders and moved the food around on his plate with his fork. "There were railroad agents from America who could connect young people with jobs here, so I took advantage of the opportunity."

"How's come no one else in your family have moved here since then?" Gabe was apparently curious now about Ker's move.

"I send part of my paycheck home to my family every month so they can *stay* together. I'd love to have family with me, but I chose to help them with cash instead."

"That's true of so many immigrants who traveled to America. It was a way to give themselves, and sometimes others, a better life," Cora added. "Dagmar's family was able to leave Sweden and move to Texas, because a rancher offered to pay their passage in exchange for working for him."

"My parents came from Ireland, too," Darcie added. "You'll hear several languages in towns in this area."

"It's not that way in Rochester," Gabe said. "You don't hear different languages where we lived. Everything is built a century or more ago, big trees, no backwards people."

Cora laughed. "Cities back East were as primitive and wild back when they started as Kansas towns are now. Think of it as getting to live in the frontier, Gabe."

"Well, I hope I get to see my sister again before ten years have passed," Gabe grumbled while looking down at his plate.

Darcie wanted to put an arm around Gabe's shoulders. Not only was Gabe taken from Rochester, but Reuben had to leave him on his own while on the cattle drive.

"You don't have to cross a sea to see your sister again," Ker reminded him. "Your pa will be sure you keep in touch. He's a good man, one you can count on." Ker pointed his fork at Gabe to make the point.

Darcie and Cora looked at each other at the same time. Reuben was a good man, but would he be able to give Gabe the love and guidance the young man needed?

"You know, Gabe, you can talk to any of us, anytime, if you're wanting to talk about your family or the situation you find yourself in. And if not someone on the ranch, talk to Pastor Reagan. He'll keep any conversation between the two of you," Darcie said, trying to steer Gabe in the right direction in case he wanted to talk to someone about his step–father.

"Talk to your horse," Jim gruffly said. "That way you'll hear yourself think out loud and figure it out yourself."

All the men nodded in unison and went back to eating. Darcie didn't think Jim's advice was the answer, but then women tended to overthink the situation at times. Maybe she should use this tactic to figure out if she should marry again and to whom. Reuben's face flashed in her mind and she blushed at her thoughts. Why was she thinking of him so much these days? Probably because of Tate gravitating to Reuben, but she had to admit she was wanting to turn to him, too.

The next morning

"Darcie, could you go into town this morning when Jim takes Gabe in for his visit? I'm hungry for those dill pickles the mercantile carries and I'd like you to get two jars of them besides some other supplies," Cora asked as she buttered her piece of toasted bread. It was the only thing she'd been eating for breakfast the last two weeks.

"Oh, of course. I didn't know Gabe was visiting someone…" Darcie fished for more information because no one had mentioned it to her.

"Yes, he's spending a few days in town while Reuben is gone," Cora replied. Darcie looked at Gabe, but he looked like he knew about it.

"Where are you staying, Gabe?" Darcie wanted to pull him in on the conversation. He sat on the end of the kitchen table eating oatmeal and pancakes which Darcie had made for everyone's breakfast this morning.

"Your father's boarding house, although I'll spend time at the Pastor's and marshal's houses for meals," Gabe responded after swallowing his food and setting his fork on his plate. Hopefully, Tate would pick up on Gabe's good table manners.

"Did Reuben know about this?" Why had she been kept out of the loop? Because she didn't have any reason to know, she guessed.

"Didn't he mention it to you?" Cora asked. "He decided it would work best for Gabe to stay in town to meet people while he's gone, then Gabe will come back to the ranch when Reuben returns."

"Makes sense."

"Why don't you take Tate into town, too?" Cora leaned closer to Darcie to whisper. "Ask if Tate could stay a few days with your father and Flora. Maybe Tate wouldn't be as jealous if he spent some time with Gabe without you or Reuben around?"

Darcie hated to be away from her son for a few days, but Tate was used to staying with family members and would get along fine. And watching Tate—ready to launch a spoonful of oatmeal at Gabe—maybe Cora's idea would help Tate accept Gabe. This rivalry was getting old.

She'd have to warn Flora to keep an eye on Gabe's boots though. Three days ago, Tate put pebbles in Gabe's boots. Gabe didn't find the little rocks until he shoved his foot into the boot. Gabe figured out who did the prank when Tate tattled on himself.

Day before yesterday, Gabe shoved his foot into…an egg, which Tate had dropped into his boot. Not only did Gabe hear the crunch of the egg shell, he could feel the smashed yolk soak into his sock when he pulled his boot on.

It *was* funny to see Gabe pull his socked foot out, but she didn't dare laugh when Tate was clearly the prankster. Gabe's sock was covered with bits of egg shells and tinted a dark yellow but what a mess to clean up when Gabe took after a screaming Tate. Unfortunately, her son wasn't old enough to clean the smeared egg footprints off the wooden floor in the bunkhouse, or else he would have done it. He did get a "sit down and listen" talk about not doing that again because it made a mess and it wasted food.

Gabe poured water into his boot to get most of the egg out. Per her suggestion, he rubbed the inside with a soapy rag, then rinsed again. Yesterday the boot was wet to wear but Gabe didn't have another pair of boots to wear. Today it was stiff after drying overnight and starting to smell like rotten eggs.

Maybe Tate needed to spend some time with her father. The former policeman might be able to steer her son away from being a juvenile delinquent.

"Gampa! Gamma!" Tate scurried out of Darcie's arms and rushed to his grandparents as soon as Jim opened the door to the boarding house for them. Tate headed toward the back of the house to the kitchen, knowing that's where at least Flora would be.

"Hello! Hello!" her father heartily called as Tate plowed into his knees. He was sitting at the kitchen table drinking a cup of coffee. Flora was setting a plate of just–baked cookies on the table when they entered the kitchen.

"You're just in time to enjoy some warm oatmeal cookies, so have a seat everyone," Flora said as she turned to get cups off the shelf above the side table.

"We've been looking forward to your visit, Gabe. The town's small compared to what you're used to, but I think you'll find plenty to do here while your father is on his trip;" her father gave a welcoming statement to Gabe.

"Thank you, Mr. and Mrs. Donovan for hosting me," Gabe replied politely.

"No formal titles here, son. Please call us Grandpa and Grandma like Tate —and every other kid in town—calls us. You'll confuse Tate, otherwise." By now, Tate was on his grandpa's lap and reaching for an oatmeal cookie.

"Gabe, do you want coffee, hot tea or milk?" Flora asked, treating him like one of her boarding house guests.

"Um, may I have some coffee?" Gabe asked timidly.

"Of course you can. Would you like cream and sugar in it, too?"

"Please and thank you."

Darcie was amused. Tate was watching Flora and Gabe talk, and not making a fuss about it. Maybe it *was* a good idea for the boys to spend time together, without her or Reuben around.

"Would it be too much for Tate to stay with you a few days, too?" she timidly asked.

"That's a great idea. Tate can introduce Gabe to Henry and Homer." Her father looked over to Gabe. "They were Tate's unofficial babysitters when Tate lived in town with Millie and Adam. The older gentlemen spend most of their day, during good weather, sitting on the bench in front of the mercantile, so they see and hear everything that goes on around town.

"You'll spend time with the Wilersons, too. You've heard Tate mention he wants a Baker's Kiss cookie? Millie, started that game, so be warned he'll want you to play, too," Flora smiled, figuring Gabe would be eating cookies and get powdered sugar all over him if Tate had his way.

"Unca Adam has doggie 'n kitty," Tate added to the conversation, since the pets were added to the family to keep Tate happy when he lived with Adam and Millie.

Her little boy was growing up fast. Before she knew it, he'd be Gabe's age. It made her sad for Reuben, knowing what he'd lost by not staying in Rochester after he recovered from the war.

What would she regret in the future if she didn't do something about it? Finding a father for her children immediately came to mind, and maybe to marry again. Reuben was the first person who came to mind for both roles. Maybe she needed to go find a horse—or dog—and talk it out.

Sunday morning

Darcie was surprised when she met her family in church this morning. Everyone was happy, not worn out from having Gabe and Tate with them for four days. She thought Tate would miss her and Amelia so much someone would have to bring him back to the ranch. Instead, her son was holding Gabe's hand, hopping up and down as they approached the pew where Darcie sat waiting for them.

"Momma!" Tate yelled as he let go of Gabe's hand and crawled into her lap while she re-settled Amelia to be able to hold both of them in her arms. Oh, how she had missed her son, but it looked like he did fine staying with her family.

"Did you have a good time with Grandpa and Grandma?"

"Yep."

"What did you do this week in town?"

"Me 'n brother played with doggy. Cat ran away," Tate looked up at her, seriously stating his last thought, but she was still on his first. *Me and brother?*

Darcie expected Gabe to sit in their pew, but he walked up the aisle and crowded in with the Reagan boys. Looks like Gabe felt comfortable sitting with friends now instead of family.

Darcie narrowed her eyes when Millie slid in next to her and automatically reached for Amelia. Darcie held both her children a little tighter, wanting some answers first. "What did you do to Tate and Gabe this week? Why are they now brothers?" she hissed at her sister.

"I don't know. I'm guessing Gabe misses his sister, and Tate realizes it is fun to have a big brother. Tate knows other children in church who have older brothers, so it was natural he wants one, too." Millie shrugged her shoulders, but Darcie was sure there was more to it than that.

Flora and her father moved into the pew from the other side and sat down beside Darcie.

"Hello, Amelia. Grandma missed you this week," Flora sweet talked to the baby, while holding out her hands, waiting for Amelia to change laps.

"Hello, Flora. Thank for your taking care of Tate…and Gabe these last few days. Any problems?" Darcie hinted. Surely it wasn't peaceful the whole time the children stayed at the boarding house.

"Your father set the rules the first hour and there were no major problems, other than what a normal two–year–old can cause," Flora smiled down at Amelia while she talked. "Ennis has handled so many situations in his career as a policeman—and as a father—that nothing fazes him."

Darcie leaned forward to talk to her father. "I need to know what you did to control fights so I can use the same tactic on Tate and Amelia," she whispered so the people around then didn't hear her.

"Firm voice, firm hand. But only go that route after you let them try to solve the problem between themselves first." Her father said it like it was the most logical thing in the world and why didn't she know that?

Tate gave Amelia a kiss when he first crawled in Darcie's lap, but then shoved her toward Flora when the older lady put her hands out to Amelia. Okay, things were back to normal between her two children. But she couldn't help but wonder how things would go in the future with Tate latching on to Gabe.

What would Reuben say when he finds out their sons are now thick as little thieves?

CHAPTER 6

Reuben had always enjoyed cattle drives, even if they moved at a slow pace. It gave him time to forget his past and just think about taking care of the cattle and the drovers. It was a short trip this time, but the nine days they had been gone seemed like weeks. Because now he had Gabe to come home to this trip…and he had to confess he thought of Darcie and her kids just as much.

Cate and Isaac made subtle hints about marriage enough times that Reuben was seriously considering talking to Darcie about getting married—for the sake of their children, of course.

But…

He'd been alone for years and was not always the best company. Reuben was used to a quiet evening after work, instead a houseful of noisy children.

His job as cook and caretaker of the ranch hands was a typical bachelor's job where you got a room to live in while you cooked and washed for a group of men. Reuben wasn't sure the pay would be enough to support a wife and three children, plus they'd need a large place to live.

Maybe it was too far a stretch to hope Darcie would even consider a marriage with him. Could she love him after the disaster of her marriage, or would she be fearful if Reuben tried to touch her?

Could Gabe and her children accept each other? Would she want more children and how would that affect Gabe and his sister, Mary?

But, he needed to consider Gabe as his first priority, no matter his feelings for Darcie. What if Gabe was so homesick here he wanted to go back to Rochester? Would Reuben move back, too, to stay in his son's life? He felt his pulse quicken, thinking about moving to a crowded city again. Because of his time in Andersonville, he sought open spaces, free of anything that felt like an enclosure.

He hadn't spent enough time with Gabe yet to know his relationship with his mother. Reuben guessed Gabe had been closer to his step–father than Mattie had liked him to be because it pulled Ringwald away from her and their daughter.

They descended down the last hill leading to the ranch yard. The normal activity of the animals and people living and working on the land eased his soul.

Even though it wasn't his property, it still felt like home to him. The headquarters of the Bar E Ranch were tucked into the base of three adjoining hills, right along a creek with springs which gave the barn and house their water source. Besides the huge stone barn and the two–story stone house, the yard held other wooden buildings: a wash house, shop, storage shed, chicken house and the bunkhouse for the ranch hands.

"Boy am I glad to be home. The money in my pocket from the cattle sale doesn't compare to coming home to Cora. I'm going on down. We'll help you unload after I kiss my wife," Dagmar grinned before giving his horse a kick in the sides to change his speed.

Reuben tried to keep a steady pace, not wanting to upset the wagon, but the horses picked up speed anyway knowing they were almost back to their own barn.

Huh. Interesting to see Gabe, Tate and the dogs running around like they were playing together. Reuben saw the moment the boys realized the group was home. Both waved at the wagon, then turned to run to the house, probably to tell Darcie and Cora the crew was home.

The women and children were at the barn by the time Reuben halted the team. Zach and Peter had put the extra horses in the corral by the barn and taken the three horses into the barn to unsaddle them. Dagmar had his arms wrapped around Cora, holding her off the ground as he kissed her, oblivious to the hands standing around them chuckling at their affection.

"I'll take the team, Reuben," Eli called out as he strolled toward the wagon. "You got family wanting to welcome you home, too." Reuben looked the direction Eli had pointed and felt a jolt in his chest. Standing near the barn door was Darcie holding Amelia, and Gabe holding a happy-looking Tate. And they all had smiles on their faces. Reuben climbed down off the wagon and stretched his legs a bit before walking over to the little group.

"Poppa Reubie!" Tate launched out of Gabe's arms when Reuben was close enough to catch him. It felt so good to have the toddler's arms wrap around his neck. He met Gabe's eyes to gauge his mood, and found that he was smiling, too.

"Welcome home, Reuben," Darcie said cheerfully, slowly swaying back and forth to keep Amelia soothed.

"Hello everybody. It's good to be back. How did things go while I was gone?" Reuben met Darcie's eyes to watch her silent answer, but she smiled and nodded her head as if to say "just fine." He was expecting her to frown, roll her eyes or purse her lips at the trouble Gabe had been while Reuben was gone.

"Glad you're back," Gabe finally said, "but we've been okay, haven't we, Tate?" Gabe lightly tickled the back of Tate's neck, causing the child to giggle and scrunch up his neck.

"Brother and me stay at Gamma's," Tate declared. *Brother and me?*

"You did? What did you do in town?"

"Played ball, visited people. Ate several pieces of Aunt Millie's delicious pies, didn't we, Tate?" Gabe replied, while teasing

Tate's neck again. Instead of pulling away, Tate launched himself into Gabe's arms, screaming in delight at Gabe's play.

"Why don't you two go help pull things out of the wagon while I talk to Darcie," he suggested to Gabe. Reuben watched them go to the back of the wagon before facing Darcie.

"*'Brother and me stayed at Grandma's?'* I was hoping the boys would start to get along while I was gone, but I am surprised to hear they're now brothers," Reuben said quietly as he took Darcie's elbow to move them away from the group so they could speak in private.

"Well, your idea of the two of them spending time together in town without us, worked to get them to accept each other," Darcie shrugged her shoulders, conceding it had worked.

"I didn't make the suggestion they spend time together in town to anyone," Reuben denying it was his idea.

"Cora said you had arranged it, and Flora and my father were waiting for their arrival so they knew about it, too."

Reuben chuckled and looked up at the sky a minute before looking back at Darcie.

"I did nothing of the sort, but Cate mentioned *you* knew about it," Reuben raised an eyebrow, waiting to see if Darcie was innocent or not.

"No, I did not," Darcie emphatically exclaimed. "So who set this all up, and why?"

"I believe 'The Saints' have decided we should be a family, so they started by getting the boys together first."

"*What?!* Cate and Flora…are matchmaking *us* together?" Darcie's face turned a pretty shade of pink. Her eyes darted one way and then the other before meeting his eyes again. She was absentmindedly bouncing Amelia faster in her arms.

Reuben put a hand on her arm. "Slow down. You're going to make Amelia dizzy at that pace."

"I need to start lunch. I'm sure you're all ready for a good meal after being on the trail," Darcie eased away to get Reuben's hand off her arm.

"Darcie," Reuben eased his hand around her forearm again, "does the idea of us joining together for the sake of our children frighten you? I am *not* and *never will be* like your former husband," he assured her.

"I know, it's just…"

"Couldn't stand to be with me?" Reuben finished her thought, dejectedly.

"No, I'm embarrassed to say *I have* thought about it." Then she whirled around and started walking briskly to the bunkhouse.

Reuben watched her leave, then turned his attention to Gabe and Tate. Gabe had changed while Reuben had been gone. His pale skin had a healthier color to it now, and his cheeks were filling out. Apparently sunshine, outdoor activities and simple home–cooked meals was a good change for his son. And it gave Reuben another painful reminder that he should have visited Gabe years ago. Maybe, with Darcie's help, he could improve the lives of three children.

It was nice to sit down on a real chair, have his plate and cup on a table, and not have to cook the meal for all the hungry cowboys. Reuben was more than happy to have Darcie in charge of the meal today. Gabe shyly grinned when Darcie said he'd helped her make the meal.

She had short notice to prepare the meal since they'd arrived before lunch, but she stretched the meal to accommodate everyone. The hot chicken and dumplings she'd fixed for lunch was piled on top of mashed potatoes. She'd opened jars of canned green beans to add a vegetable to the meal because she didn't have time to pick, snap and boil the beans still growing in the garden. Darcie's soda biscuits were soft, fluffy and much better than his. Melted butter and currant jelly dripped between his fingers as he ate his third biscuit, but he quickly licked his fingers not wanting to waste the sweet topping. He couldn't wait to see what she had made for dessert.

Lunch in the bunkhouse could almost be labeled a joyous affair. The cowboys were tired from their long days in the saddle and being out in the weather full–time, but now they were happy swapping stories of what had happened on the trail and here on the ranch.

"We only had one evening storm we thought would scatter the herd, but luckily the clouds moved on before completely drenching us," Zach said between scooping mashed potatoes in his mouth.

"That was a gentle sprinkle compared to the weather I've experienced on past drives, Zach," Dagmar scoffed. "I remember one lightning bolt that hit so fast and close we were all deaf for a few days. The bolt hit one of the metal stakes we'd pounded into the ground to tie a rope around to make a temporary corral for the horses," Dagmar explained.

Gabe was hanging on every word being said around the table. "What happened then?"

"Oh, it was bad," Dagmar looked down at his plate and shook his head. "Every critter took off at breakneck speed away from the bolt's point of contact. I won't go into detail with T–A–T–E at the table, but we lost over a hundred head of stock, two hands, and the chuck wagon was a pile of fire wood after a thousand head of cattle ran over it. Took three days to round up the scattered herd which had run several miles in opposite directions. It was by God's protection we didn't lose anyone in our immediate family."

"How long ago was this?" Zach asked.

"Let's see. It was before the War, and we were driving a herd to Baton Rouge..."

"That's in Louisiana," Gabe interrupted.

"It is. We'd round up wild cattle in Texas and drive them wherever they needed beef. I've been through several states and territories though the years."

"How old were you when this bad storm happened?" Peter asked.

"Leif would have been about fourteen or fifteen, me two years younger, and I don't think the twins were even eleven at the time.

"You were my age?!" Gabe squawked with the realization.

"Yep, riding in the middle of a thundering herd, in the pouring rain—pitch black except when the lightning lit up the sky. Dreading the moment I was gonna be knocked down and trampled by the panicking cattle. Or, getting hit by the next lightning bolt," Dagmar was getting into his story.

"T–A–T–E is starting to figure out some of your conversation, Dagmar," Cora stopped her husband's story.

"So, yeah, we just had a sprinkle of rain on this trip. Cate and Isaac enjoyed the trail drive, then boarded the train leading to the next leg of their adventure," Dagmar concluded and went back to eating.

"When do they plan to be back home?" Darcie asked.

"In a month, in time for your...ouch!" Dagmar stopped talking and leaned over to rub his shin. "Did you just...oh, never mind," when he saw Reuben glaring at him from across the table.

"What's for dessert, Darcie?" Reuben switched tactics to get off the subject Dagmar almost spilled to her and everyone at the table.

She looked confused a moment but then answered, "I made cream puffs for the few of us who were going to be at lunch today, so you'll only get one each now..."

Darcie rolled her eyes and waited to talk again when the men all let out a disappointing groan. "So I made rice pudding to go with it."

"*Tack så mycket!* Thank you for making my favorite dessert, Darcie! Did you make *kräm* for it, too?" Dagmar's eyes shined under his raised eyebrows.

"I'm sorry, Dagmar, I didn't have time to make the grape juice sauce you like to eat with it. But I have strawberry preserves to spoon on the pudding and cream puff. Will that do?"

Another round of contented talk went around the table. You'd think Reuben had never made a dessert for these guys the way they acted. Of course, it could be an act to compliment Darcie.

"We've been eating this good since Darcie took over the cooking," Eli pointed out. "Yesterday noon, Darcie served a chicken pie, deviled eggs, a sour cream cake that would beat her sister's version in a competition—and you know how good a baker Millie is."

"Last night's dessert was a raisin cream pie," Ker added.

"My favorite so far has been the lemon chiffon pie," Gabe added, getting into the spirit of praising Darcie's cooking.

"Cookies!" Tate yelled, making the men chuckle. Gosh, this had been a sober bunch of cowboys before Darcie and her kids took over the bunkhouse. Good food, a bunkhouse decorated like a home, and children to brighten their day. No wonder the ranch hands were happy to work here now. Bet she'd washed and ironed their shirts better than he did, too.

Was he mad that Darcie was taking better care of the bunkhouse and crew than he'd been doing? No, when he thought about it. Instead of doing the cooking, he was ready to go home at the end of the day to a wife who was a good cook, and a family to brighten and share his life. Maybe it was time to move forward with his life instead of keeping it the way it had been since the war.

CHAPTER 7

Meet me at the porch swing tonight after you get the children to sleep. We need to talk.

That's all Reuben had said before she left the bunkhouse this afternoon. He fed the hands supper in the bunkhouse tonight, and she made a special meal in the house kitchen for Cora and Dagmar's reunion meal. Darcie and her children ate in the kitchen to leave the couple to themselves. Gabe opted to eat with the men, which she was glad he did. He and his father needed time together now that Reuben was back on the ranch.

The evening was hot, but Darcie could feel the heat lessening as the sun sank below the horizon. At least there was a nice breeze most evenings. So different from the muggy nights in Chicago. The tenement houses were too close together the get a breeze through them.

She used her foot to slowly rock the porch swing back and forth as she waited for Reuben.

Yipper laid on the porch near the steps, her tongue lolling out of her mouth as she kept watch on her world. Dagmar had said Yipper preferred to guard her people. Kipper tended to stay close to the barn and the stock instead. Kind of like women take care of the hearth and home and men protect and provide.

Reuben caught her daydreaming when he walked up the steps. She'd been facing the bunkhouse and hadn't seen him walk across the yard. Darcie put her foot down on the floor to stop the motion of the swing, then scooted over so Reuben could sit on the other side of the swing. He did so, but started the swing again without saying a word.

Darcie finally had to break the silence. "You said you wanted to talk?" Darcie fished for information about why he asked to meet with her.

"Would you mind if we went for a walk so we can talk away from the buildings? I don't want Gabe to overhear us," Reuben softly asked and explained.

"Oh, of course, that's fine." Reuben stood and held out his hand, waiting for her to take his before walking down the steps and east, away from the buildings. She didn't mind when he tucked her hand around his elbow while they strolled. It made her feel safe instead of uneasy.

"Gabe has adjusted better than I ever thought possible when we left Rochester, and it happened when I was away on the cattle drive."

"Well, you know when Cate and Flora plan something, it usually works out for the best. Having the boys spend time with my father and Flora seemed to help smooth over their jealousy a bit. They are dear women, but sometimes it worries me what they might do next," Darcie chuckled.

"Well, Cate filled me in on their next plan—for us—when I was out on the drive with them."

"And is it…good or bad?"

"It could be either way, depending on what you think, and how it would affect our children," Reuben glanced her way, but the evening shadows were making it hard to see his facial expressions.

"How am I going to take care of Gabe has been constantly on my mind since we left Rochester. I have a secure job, and the wages are enough to get me by, but I live in a bunkhouse with other men instead of a house. Gabe should be continuing school in town instead of being isolated on the ranch. I could teach him at home, but he is already way past the simple schooling I have had."

They continued to walk a distance before Reuben stopped and turned toward her. "I've been thinking about this, then Cate laid it out plain and simple to me. So, I'm going to do the same to you, so we can rationally talk about it."

"What's 'it'?" Darcie wondered what he was leading up to. Reuben dropped her hand and wiped his hands down his face, then through his dark hair since he hadn't worn his hat.

"We've both been married so we can talk frankly about this. I realize you may have reservations about marrying again because of your bad marriage."

Darcie wrapped her arms around her middle, thinking of what she'd endured while married to Curtis. Why hadn't she left him, rather than put up with it? Because he was a policeman, she had no money, she was in physical and mental pain... She squeezed her eyes to stop the memories.

When Darcie married Curtis Robbins over three years ago she thought he loved and cherished her and the children they'd have together. He was so attentive, always needed to be with her, made the decisions for their wedding and future, and Darcie thought it was wonderful to have a strong husband to provide for her.

Turns out he was an obsessive, abusive husband—verbally, then physically abusing her. She tried to be perfect so he couldn't find any fault, but Curtis kept finding new things to belittle her for instead of complimenting her for doing her best, while often in pain from the last round he'd meted out to her.

Darcie was too embarrassed and ashamed to tell her father, a policeman, that her husband, also working for the Chicago police, was treating her in this manner. It didn't help that Curtis was always wonderful to her father and sister Millie.

She realized Reuben was talking again so she concentrated on his voice to pull her out of her thoughts.

"No woman should go through what you did with a man; but marriage can be a good thing and I'd hope you'll consider what I'm about to say."

Then it stuck her, "Do you realize we've talked more since you returned from Rochester—even with you gone nine days—than we had in the past months?"

"Yes, and I apologize for it. I've been so bitter about life—until I went back to Rochester to face my past."

"And now that you did, you're wondering what to do next," Darcie now had an inkling of where this was headed, but it didn't scare her as much as she thought it might.

"I don't want to say anything to anyone else, including our children, until we thoroughly talk this out." Reuben took a deep breath. "People often marry for the sake of their families. A man marries the woman taking care of his children to save her reputation since they would be living in the same house. A widower marries his brother's widow to combine households.

"Would you consider us getting married, for the sake of our children? Then they'd have two parents, and a much better future."

She paused to collect her thoughts before answering his life–changing question. "It has crossed my mind my children would be better taken care of if I marry again."

"Anyone, or possibly to me?"

"Our friends and family have been pushing us together for some time, so they must think we're compatible."

"Even though we've disagreed about tasks around the Bar E?" Reuben questioned.

"I believe that was because *the man* felt threatened—or jealous—of *the woman* stepping into his territory," Darcie countered but didn't say any more when Reuben stepped closer.

She froze a second, but then relaxed as Reuben slowly ran his big, calloused hands up and down her upper arms. "And I apologize for that.

"Would you want a real marriage, or just the ceremony to make it legal?"

"For now, I'd be more comfortable with convenience." Darcie missed his touch as soon as he dropped his hands to his side.

"But, that could change if I felt safe and comfortable."

"So, your answer is…" She heard him hold his breath.

And Darcie exhaled the breath she was holding. "I'll think about it, for our children's sakes."

"Okay, let's talk this out more," Reuben sounded relieved she hadn't flatly turned him down. He commenced to pace in front of her as he planned his next words.

Not quite the romantic scene she had when Curtis proposed. He was down on one knee, staring up at her in admiration, she romantically dreaming of the wonderful marriage they'd have. Yes, better to think of this marriage as practical instead of romantic.

"We'd be all right financially, as I have some money in the bank. I started from scratch eight years ago, but I've always had a job that included room and board. The trip to Rochester is the only thing I've spent money on.

"Next thing is where to live." Reuben stopped walking to concentrate on her face.

Darcie pushed down the bad memories of living with Curtis in their home. "I'm sure we could keep our same quarters we each have now, but that would confuse the children if they weren't living together as a family, with their parents in the same house.

"I'll talk to Cora and Dagmar about it. I'm sure they'd prefer us to stay on the ranch or close by. I suppose we could rent a house in Clear Creek and I could ride back and forth. If we had bad weather or have problems on the ranch, I could stay in the bunkhouse."

Darcie had to ask the question looming in her mind. "*If* we went through with your marriage idea, when would we marry?"

Reuben cleared his throat. "Cate suggested a month from last Sunday because she and Isaac would be back from their trip," he replied in a teasing voice, "but she gave us permission to marry sooner if we preferred."

Darcie watched the smile that spread over Reuben's face, and she caught herself thinking she'd like to kiss it. Reuben wasn't what you'd call a handsome man, but his emotions truthfully played across his features.

Darcie had learned Curtis's handsome face masked the anger which was always ready to erupt. He might have had a smile on his lips but a slight narrowing of his left eye caused her spine to tremble.

"*If* we get married," Reuben's words pulled her out of her bad thoughts, "would you want the ceremony after church with the congregation present, or just us and Pastor?"

Visions of her wedding in the Cathedral in Chicago flashed through her mind and she involuntarily shivered from the memory. It was a happy event at the time, but the marriage soon became a distorted nightmare.

But she knew exactly what kind of man she'd be marrying in Reuben. He was a decent, hardworking man, kind and gentle with her children. Darcie knew she could *always* trust him, and right now that meant more to her than love.

"Oh, I forgot to tell you what Tate told me right before we left on the drive," Reuben chuckled. "After I gave you a kiss to satisfy Tate, he whispered we were then married since we kissed."

"Oh, the little squirt. He never told me that!"

"So he'll expect us to kiss, like the other newlywed couples around us."

"But we'd marry for our children's sakes, not love. I don't want to mislead him in assuming it's a real marriage."

"If we marry, I'm forever committed to you and your children. In that way, it is—and always will be—a real marriage. Kissing is a way to show and teach children there is respect between partners and a family. Did Tate see that in your first marriage?"

Darcie looked down to the ground and sadly shook her head. "All he saw and felt was pain when Curtis touched us." She took a deep breath to wash away those memories. "Millie and Adam taught Tate love through cookies and kisses."

"So…supporting and teaching our children how to love would be the priority in our marriage, and maybe we'd learn to love each other along the way, too."

Darcie took in a deep breath, then exhaled it. She touched Reuben's arm to have him turn toward her.

She had been thinking about accepting his marriage proposal, and Reuben's last words helped to make up her mind. He sounded sincere and it would be so easy to fall in love with the man.

CHAPTER 8

Reuben couldn't believe how much life had changed for all of them when Darcie accepted his proposal.

He was nervous walking into church as a family after they decided to marry. Gabe walked down the aisle first, then Darcie carrying Amelia and him holding Tate, claiming a section of pew for their newly–formed family. But Reuben shouldn't have been worried what the congregation thought about their arrival. When Pastor Reagan announced their pending wedding in a month, people actually clapped for them, and congratulated him and Darcie after the service.

Gabe was genuinely happy with their decision, looking forward to being a family with him, along with Darcie's brood. Sounded like the maid took care of him and his sister more than Mattie. They had talked about taking the family to Rochester to meet his sister in early spring, so Gabe freely talked about Mary now without pain in his eyes.

Peter had been the right person to teach Gabe to ride, and proper care of his horse and equipment. Now Gabe blended in with the cowboys riding the range because of his attire and tanned face. Work clothes bought the first week in Kansas were getting short and tight, indicating Gabe was growing like a weed.

Reuben loved Tate and Amelia like they were his own children. He felt so blessed he'd get to watch and help them grow up after missing Gabe's formative years. Tate and Amelia fussed now if they thought they hadn't had their fair share of Reuben's time. There were tears as well as giggles, like a real family would have.

But Darcie surprised him the most. Knowing she'd have help raising her children lifted a big weight off her shoulders. She smiled more, teased him and the children about things with a sparkle in her eye. Darcie reached for his hand now and gave it a squeeze.

The women in the Wilerson and Hamner families were working on wedding plans. Reuben didn't care what kind of cake Millie would make for the reception, but it was an important decision for the women to discuss, along with flowers and the dresses for her and Amelia.

Every time Darcie asked a question or shared something, she beamed at him, and Reuben felt ten feet tall. He was falling in love with Darcie and couldn't wait to share their lives together.

Now he and Darcie were in Clear Creek for a legal matter that needed to be taken care of. Cora's brother, Lyle Elison, had recently moved from Boston to Clear Creek to practice law.

Lyle was here for Cora's and Dagmar's wedding, then returned to Boston to apprentice at a law firm. When Lyle was ready to strike out on his own, he decided to practice in Kansas. He rented the building next to Clancy's Café, using the downstairs as his office and living in the upstairs rooms.

Reuben opened the office door, then stepped back to allow Darcie to enter first. They could have gone to the lawyer in Ellsworth, but wanted to patronize the new lawyer in town, especially since Lyle was his boss's brother.

The space had been divided into three sections. The first being a reception area with chairs and a desk for a receptionist. Lyle hadn't hired anyone yet as he didn't have enough business to require help. The second room was Lyle's office for private consultation, and the back room so far was empty.

"Hello, Reuben and Darcie. Please come into the office and have a seat." Lyle stepped out of his office and motioned to enter.

After Reuben seated Darcie, Lyle went around his desk and sat in his upholstered swivel chair.

"Thank you, Lyle. I've been anxious to see what you found," Darcie got right to the point. It had been two weeks since they met with Lyle the first time, and she wanted news.

Lyle nervously looked at Reuben and cleared his throat. Reuben thought Lyle had a lot of gumption to work in Clear Creek after all the shenanigans he and his friends pulled when Lyle and Carl lived on the Bar E Ranch a few years ago. His parents sent their sons here to work on the ranch to give them something to do, but they didn't do a lick of work.

Reuben decided to give Lyle a chance to redeem himself by filing the paperwork for the children's adoptions, plus Lyle insisted to do it free, being it was his first case as a full–fledged lawyer.

"Darcie, I've filed the paperwork for Reuben to adopt Tate and Amelia. The judge will have no problem granting this because you are divorced from Mr. Robbins, and he's in jail for murder. You have already named your sister Millie as your children's guardian, and I suggest you leave that in place in case something should happen to both of you," Lyle looked to Darcie for her consent.

"Is that all right, Reuben?" Darcie turned to ask.

Reuben thought for a moment. "Since Millie's married now, should you list both her and Adam as guardians?"

"Oh yes, excellent idea. I'll add Marshal Wilerson's name." Lyle met Reuben's eyes but his face flushed a little, probably embarrassed he hadn't suggested it before Reuben. Lyle dipped his pen in the inkwell and scribbled on a piece of paper, apparently as a note to change the guardianship.

"Have you heard back from my former wife about Darcie adopting Gabe?" Reuben knew it was a longshot that Mattie would relinquish her rights to her firstborn, but Reuben wanted to check out the matter.

"I've sent two telegrams as you suggested to speed up the process, one to Mrs. Ringwald, and the other to the lawyer who you said was handling Mr. Ringwald's estate."

"And?" Reuben was holding his breath, because Mattie was holding the cards so to speak.

"You knew I received a telegraph back from the lawyer, Mr. Abercrombie, acknowledging my inquiry and that he would meet with Mrs. Ringwald. I have not received more correspondence from him, but hopefully something in writing will arrive in the mail soon," Lyle reported. "I never heard back from Mrs. Ringwald, nor did I expect to, assuming instead any response would come from their family attorney."

"So now what should we do about Gabe's protection?"

"It would depend on whether his mother had already listed guardians. At least he is old enough to fend for himself, if he really needed to, but I would still recommend having the Marshal and Millie listed as his guardians until age eighteen."

"Good idea. Check with the Wilersons first to ensure whether it is okay though."

"I can list them as guardians while in Kansas, but his mother would have to be notified in case she already has named guardians for Gabe."

"Will any of this delay our marriage?" Darcie asked Lyle.

"No, you should be able to go ahead with your plans and the paperwork will fall into place later."

Reuben stood, reached across the desk to pump Lyle's hand. After years of heartache, he and Gabe were finally together, ready to start a new family with Darcie and her children.

CHAPTER 9

It couldn't be her. *Mattie* was standing on the ranch house porch next to Darcie? Reuben gritted his teeth to control the angry words ready to erupt from his mouth. He knew she was up to some trick, showing up unannounced.

Reuben, Dagmar and Gabe had left at dawn to move a group of cattle to a new section of grass while the morning was still cool. Now back late morning, Reuben continued to the barn, planning to take care of his horse before confronting Mattie.

"*That's mother!* What's she doing here?" Gabe twisted around in his saddle to stare at the women on the porch, but followed Reuben into the barn.

"Don't know. Maybe she decided you needed to go back home. What's your choice on the subject before we go meet her? Stay here or go back to Rochester?"

Reuben hated to be blunt with his son, but he was old enough to decide what to do. He had bonded with his son, so no matter where Gabe lived, he'd be sure they'd stay connected by letters and hopefully visits.

"I miss Mary, but life is so much easier living here with you. I don't know what to say." Gabe swung off his horse, then looked toward the house before tugging the horse's reins to enter the barn.

Dust motes danced in the air as they entered the dim interior of the center of the barn.

"You know the woman on the porch?" Dagmar followed behind Reuben and Gabe with his mount.

"That's Gabe's mother, but I have no idea why she's here."

"I'll take care of your horses so you can go meet her," Dagmar offered.

"Nope, we're going to take care of our horses, and she can wait, or come down to the barn." His horse stepped sideways in protest when Reuben yanked the leather to unhook the cinch. "And we're going to rub down the horses, feed them oats before letting them out into the corral, and we might even get out the saddle soap and give the bridles and saddles a good cleaning." *How dare she come to Clear Creek? She kicked Gabe out of the house and now she shows up?*

"Think she came by herself?" Gabe asked as he pulled the saddle off his horse, thinking of his sister.

"Would she leave Mary with the maid and cook?"

"She and Reginald took trips now and then, leaving us at home with the help, so I can see Mother leaving her behind."

"You know you're leaving Darcie up there to play hostess to her," Dagmar pointed out. "Cora was going to spend the day at Rania's house so she's not home."

Reuben knocked back his hat and rubbed his hand over his face to wipe off the sweat and settle his mind. "Okay, we better get up there then. We'll get back to work as soon as we can."

"Don't worry about it. You've got to deal with some family issues, so that trumps mucking stalls."

"Nope, I'd rather shovel horse manure than meet with Mattie. Sorry, Gabe, I shouldn't have said that out loud," Reuben growled before putting his arm across Gabe's shoulder and pulling him toward the barn entrance.

He couldn't tell which woman looked more steamed— Mattie, because he and Gabe had taken their sweet time leaving the barn instead of galloping to the porch as soon as they spotted her—

or Darcie. She stood ramrod straight with Amelia on her hip and her other hand tightly holding a fidgeting Tate.

Gabe stayed by his side when Reuben stopped six feet away from the porch steps. Reuben widened his stance and folded his arms across his chest, waiting for Mattie, or Darcie, to say something.

"Gabriel. I'm…glad to see you. Are you enjoying *playing cowboy* with your father?" Mattie's arms were crossed too, over a gray silk gown. So much for wearing widow black to mourn Ringwald's demise.

"Yes I am, actually." Reuben was proud of Gabe's mature conversation with his mother.

"So what's your reason for this visit, Mattie?" Reuben glanced at Darcie and he could have sworn there was steam rising from her red hair.

"I received your lawyer's telegram and talked to my own counsel," Mattie rolled her shoulders back. "To put it bluntly, we're still married, Reuben." A smirking smile spread over her face as she gauged his reaction.

"But you're …" Gabe started to say before Reuben raised his hands to cut him off.

"Don't say another word about *anything*, Gabe," Reuben quietly told his son.

"Oh, yes. I got the telegram requesting I relinquish my rights to Gabriel, so you could marry your betrothed. I assume you were marrying your *maid* so your other children would be *legitimate*?" Gabe gasped and looked back at Reuben, who shook his head again to keep quiet. Darcie hadn't said a word yet. What had Mattie told Darcie when she arrived?

"Gabe is my only child, but the children on this ranch call me *'Poppa'*, since *my son* uses that endearment for me," Reuben countered.

"Well isn't that sweet you help the little urchins…"

Darcie turned on her heel and stormed for the door, pulling a protesting Tate with her. The screen door slammed as she escaped into the house. Reuben would have to talk to her later to smooth over all Mattie accused him of doing.

"So how could I still be married to you, when you had me declared *dead*?" Reuben knew she was playing some sort of tactics game with him, and his life.

"It was a technicality I found out after Reginald died."

"If we're still married, doesn't that make your children with Ringwald illegitimate?"

"That's all taken care of. You know money can buy *anything*, Rueben," Mattie rolled her eyes and did a little flip with her hand. "Now, I want you to sell this ranch, and then we can go back to Rochester."

Reuben snorted a laugh and shook his head. "You want me to sell this *six–thousand* acre ranch? Then what would I do with the *five hundred* or so head of cattle and horses that graze on this land? That's how this ranch makes its money." Mattie's eyes widened when he mentioned the size of the ranch.

"You can up the asking price of the ranch to include the animals." Mattie raised her shoulders as if it was so easy to do.

"I'd rather stay here and oversee my *vast empire*. You move here instead," Reuben countered back.

Mattie looked around the ranch yard then out to the pasture which rolled into the horizon. "No. I will not live in this god–forsaken country," she hotly replied.

"I didn't think you'd like to live out on the Kansas prairie," Reuben couldn't help badgering her.

"Swede, could you come over and meet Gabe's mother, Mrs. Ringwald?" Reuben called to Dagmar as he headed to the back entrance of the house.

Dagmar warily sauntered up to stand by Gabe and touched the brim of his hat. "Good day, ma'am."

"Well, isn't that nice. Besides your *Irish* maid, you've hired *Swedish immigrants*, too. I overheard on the train there were a lot of *them* in Kansas."

Dagmar looked at Reuben in confusion.

"You assumed wrong, Mattie. Kansas is the land of opportunity. Mr. Hamner and his wife *own* this ranch. I'm just a drover and cook here."

"You're joking," Mattie's prim voice held a hint of disdain.

"I don't appreciate you cutting down my heritage, or that of my help, Mrs. Ringwald," Dagmar's voice turned deep, and he put a hand on his hip, right above his revolver to make the point. "You are most welcome to leave *my home and ranch* at any time if you continue to be rude."

"No, it can't be true," Mattie's wide eyes darted between Reuben's and Dagmar's.

"It's public record at the county courthouse in Ellsworth who owns the Bar E Ranch, if you don't believe me or my help," Dagmar firmly stated.

"Why are you just a hired hand, Reuben? I thought they gave away free land out here," Mattie waved her hand in the general direction of the pasture.

"Yes, a person can claim one hundred sixty acres, but it takes money to build a house and barn, buy livestock and farming equipment. Remember slamming the door of our home to shut me out when I returned from the war? I only owned the ragged clothes I wore and the few dollars in my pocket. Plus, since you'd declared me dead, I haven't gotten any war pensions, but I bet you've been collecting widow's pay, haven't you?" Mattie didn't answer, but her face gave away the answer to the question he'd asked.

"So where do you live now?" She changed the subject to deflect from herself.

"See the bunkhouse over there, Mattie? I have *a room* in it, about the same size space as your foyer, which holds my bed, Gabe's cot, a small dresser, chair and small pot–bellied stove. Are you ready to live in a space that small with me and Gabe already in it? There's a hook for one spare set of clothing per person. Could you leave behind all your clothing but one dress to work in and one for church? Oh, and there would be no maid so you'd be doing all the housework yourself."

"Mr. *Ranch Owner* would have to build a house to accommodate the space we needed then."

"Sorry, Ma'am. Don't work that way. That's Reuben's living quarters whether he's single or married with a family."

"So, if we moved back to New York, your parents would be financing our family, Mattie, because my simple cowboy skills wouldn't earn enough money in downtown Rochester to maintain your lavish lifestyle," Reuben shrugged his shoulders, acting like it was okay to live off her family like they had done before.

It was interesting to see Mattie's face turn deathly pale. What was the reason behind her visit? He'd thought she'd have a big windfall of money with the passing of her husband. What happened when Ringwald died?

"So your choice, Mattie, is you move into the cook's room with me and Gabe, or divorce me—if we are indeed still married—so you can find another rich husband to finance you."

"What about my daughter?"

"Except for Gabe, I'm not responsible for Mary, Mattie. Mary would have to live with Ringwald's parents, or yours. I *assume* Mary is Reginald's child?"

Silence hung in the air as he waited for her response, but she didn't answer for several long moments.

"I put Reginald's name on Mary's birth certificate, but it could have been either of you." Mattie pronounced. "Mary looks just like me, so we'll never really know."

Reuben glanced over at Gabe, shocked this fact had to come out in front of his son, about his sister. How many other secrets had Mattie kept from her family?

"In the meantime I need a place to stay…" she glanced at the house, waiting for an offer to stay in the ranch house.

"I'm sure you'll be comfortable at the Paulson Hotel, *Mrs.* Ringwald, because we won't be accommodating you here," Dagmar said, then left before she could protest his lack of hospitality.

"Gabe, we need to get back to work," Reuben said as he turned to walk back to the barn.

"Wait a minute! What about me?"

"What about you?"

Reuben tried to keep his voice calm, but inside he was smoldering with anger at this woman. Now she'd probably mess up his life a second time, because when Darcie left the porch, she looked like she was going take her kids and run out of his life the way she did with her first marriage.

"I need a ride back to Clear Creek. I hired the man at the livery stable to bring me out here, but he went back into town," she confessed. "I…didn't think I'd be going back to town so soon."

"You going to walk, or do you want to borrow a horse? But don't try to sell it. Horse thieves get hung around here."

Good. Mattie looked sad and defeated, but she'd never feel as bad as he did the day he arrived home after the war.

"Can Gabe drive me back to town?"

"No. I won't leave you alone with him to poison his mind again."

"I'm *sorry*, Reuben, but I can't get back to town by myself. I wouldn't even know which way to walk."

"Nor are you equipped in case a prairie wolf or rattlesnake decides to attack you as you walk the miles back to town."

Reuben knew it was cruel, but he loved the sense of power; his words caused Mattie to shrink back against the porch post.

"Give me a few minutes to get a horse hitched to the buggy and I'll take you back to town," Reuben grumbled. He didn't want to sit by her for any reason, but he needed to get her off the ranch, plus talk to Lyle about her visit anyway.

"Um. While you're doing that, can I go into the house and use their toilet?" Did she really need to go, or did she want an excuse to get into the house?

"There's no plumbing on the ranch, Mattie. See the outhouse behind the bunkhouse?" he pointed to the tiny building since it could be seen from where they were standing. "That's our *toilet room*. Be sure to knock on the door before you go in because *everybody* on the ranch uses it. And watch out for snakes and spiders, too. They like to lurk in those dark, dank holes."

***

Was Reuben still married to that woman? The thought made her angrier each time it echoed in her head! Surely that wasn't right, or he wouldn't have talked about marrying her and adopting Tate and Amelia. Darcie went into the house when she couldn't bear to hear another word, although Reuben's and Mattie's raised voices flowed through the open windows of the house. Plus, Tate was getting upset, and Reuben didn't need her son to run to him during this argument with his...wife.

Dagmar came into the house cursing in Swedish. He dipped a tin cup into the pail of water by the dry sink, swallowed it in three gulps, and stomped back out the door without looking for Darcie. From the hallway, she could see Mattie still standing on the porch and Reuben and Gabe facing her, but she was too far enough away to hear their actual words.

What would happen now? Was Reuben really still married to that pompous...witch? What did he ever seen in her? Things had turned around for Darcie and her children and she was looking forward to becoming a family with Reuben and Gabe. And the worst of it was, she had fallen in love, with another woman's husband.

CHAPTER 10

Reuben hurried to hitch up the horse and buggy and found Mattie was rooted to the same spot where he left her.

He pushed the horse hard enough that the buggy wheels rattled to prevent talk and they arrived in town quicker than usual. Mattie had one hand holding her fancy hat on top of her head and the other hand clutching the side of the buggy.

"Get out," Reuben said as the buggy pulled up to the hotel.

"Aren't you going to help me down?"

"That's what the steps are for on the side of the buggy." Reuben said while looking straight ahead, waiting for the buggy to dip to the side so he could tell she was off and he could leave.

"What about my luggage?" Reuben forgot he'd shoved her carpet bag under the seat.

"Catch," he yanked it from its place, held the bag over the side of the buggy where she now stood and dropped it. She stepped back rather than catch it, so the bag knocked up a cloud of dust when it hit the ground. Too bad it hadn't landed on a pile of fresh manure.

"You're being very uncouth and rude, Reuben. *Why are you treating me this way?!"* Mattie screeched. Her face was red and screwed up in rage.

People were stopping along the boardwalk to stare at them, but Reuben didn't care who heard them at this point. He wasn't the guilty party here. "Remember locking me out of our house eight years ago, denying me to see my son, denying me shelter, food and clothing after I returned from *the War*?" He could hear people murmuring now as they caught the words.

"But I'm your wife!"

"You were, until you *paid* to have me declared *killed in battle* so you could *marry your lover!*" Reuben yelled back. He closed his eyes and took a deep breath before looking back down at her. He lowered his voice and hissed, "And since I'm dead, I'm only a ghost from your past, so there's no reason for you to come near me or my son again."

Reuben flicked the reins to get the horse to take off. He'd have to drive out of town a few miles before he was calm enough to drive back into town to talk to Lyle. Mattie had pushed him out of Gabe's life eight years ago, and he had crawled away like a coward. This time he was going to fight back because Mattie was not going to take away his future with Gabe, Darcie and her children.

Reuben pushed open the door to the lawyer's office, but stopped short when he realized Lyle had people in his office. Especially since it was people he knew. Ennis and the marshal were leaning up against the inside office wall with Millie and Darcie seated in the chairs in front of Lyle's desk.

Could he feel any worse? While he was driving around the country to cool his temper, Darcie had ridden into town, summoned her father, sister and Adam to meet with Lyle. This was his problem, but apparently Darcie had little faith in him and felt she had to fight Mattie for him.

Or were they talking about dropping Reuben's request to adopt Tate and Amelia?

"Join the discussion, Reuben," Lyle waved his hand to motion Reuben into the room. "Darcie wanted her father's input since he's a retired policeman."

Reuben took off his hat and nervously fingered the brim. "I'm so sorry, Darcie," Reuben pleaded while walking to where she sat in the room.

Darcie put up her hand, signaling for him to stop. "Don't apologize to me, Reuben—unless you haven't been honest with me about your situation—with your wife. And if you haven't been truthful, you better make this right for our children. I won't let Tate go through the trauma of a man abusing him again," Darcie's words and glare stopped him in his tracks.

"I would never hurt Tate," Reuben pleaded.

"I know you wouldn't intentionally hurt him, but nonetheless, I have to think of him and Amelia first." She dropped her eyes to her clamped hands in her lap.

Reuben looked over to Ennis to gauge his reaction. Did Darcie's father want Reuben out of his daughter's and grandchildren's lives after Mattie showing up with her accusations?

Lyle cleared his throat. "Ennis and Adam have been giving me advice on how to proceed with Mattie's declaration she is still married to you, Reuben."

"Besides checking into your war and marriage records, I think we should inquire about the cause of Mr. Ringwald's death," Ennis added. "What were you told when you were in Rochester?"

"Just that he was found dead in his office. Doctor suggested heart failure."

"Well, something's not right if she traveled all the way out here," Ennis continued. "I assume her husband was wealthy by the look of Gabe's clothes when he arrived. Why would she want to connect with you now?"

"From a parent's standpoint, I'd assume she wants Gabe to move back home, although she didn't mention that when out to the Bar E. Just brought up our marriage."

"Did she say anything about her daughter traveling with her?" Adam asked.

"Not a word," Rueben shook his head, but he looked around the room when no one else said anything. "Why?"

"I saw them get off at the depot together. Ethan Paulson confirmed there is a young daughter with Mrs. Ringwald," Adam stated.

Reuben squeezed his eyes shut and tightened his jaw in anger. "She'll use Mary as a ploy to pull Gabe home. Then she'd hope I follow them back to New York."

"At least she didn't leave her child home alone. So what is Mattie's motive when declaring you two are still married? What does she gain?" Millie questioned him.

Millie had asked the right questions when Darcie's husband had shown up in town trying to get Tate back and to have Millie arrested. It made the marshal learn to listen when the woman's intuition kicked in. Maybe she was onto something now.

Millie tented her fingers in front of her face and tapped her chin while thinking. "What is the one thing you think Mattie cares the most about, Reuben? Past or present?"

"For some reason she pushed Gabe away when she had the opportunity, but now needs him back," Darcie stated before Reuben could answer.

"Money," both sisters said at the same time.

"Girls, I believe you're on the right track," Ennis proudly stated.

"So even if Ringwald's death was natural or caused…something has come up about his will and how it pertains to Gabe and Reuben," Millie mused.

Lyle sat at his desk, apparently not wanting to interrupt Millie, Darcie and Ennis as they talked about the problem Lyle and Reuben should be talking about privately. No, this time Reuben needed to rely on his friends and counsel. The more people involved in this, the sooner the problem with Mattie could be solved. Slinking away instead of standing up to Mattie last time had caused Reuben to miss years of his son's life.

"Lyle, as a former policeman who has solved more cases than your age, I suggest we work together to wire and write to everyone we can think of to solve this case. I want my daughter and grandchildren happy and safe, and I stand behind Darcie choosing Reuben to do both," Ennis pushed away from the wall and put his hat back on his head.

"Girls, you need to find a way so Mary and Gabe can safely reunite. That boy needs to see his sister."

"Divide and conquer?" Millie smiled at her father.

"More like keep your enemies close so you can keep tabs on them, Millie," Ennis answered.

"Exactly what are you suggesting, Ennis?" Reuben almost hated to ask.

"After we stop by the marshal's office so I can pick up a deputy star to pin on my vest, I suggest we all go over to the hotel to welcome Mrs. Ringwald to town. If she sees you have a lawyer plus two officers of the law beside you, she might be more hesitant to think she can get her way."

"We can use the church or our home as a place where Gabe and Mary can spend time together," Millie added. "I assume we shouldn't suggest the ranch?" She looked to Adam for his agreement, but he shrugged his shoulders like he didn't think it mattered where they met.

"How long will it take to get proof of my marriage status, Lyle?" Reuben asked.

"Could be a matter of days, or weeks dealing with the fact the paperwork we need is in New York," Lyle honestly replied.

"Think Mattie would stay here in town while we wait for proof?" Ennis asked.

"She can go wherever she wants because I don't plan to spend any time with her," Reuben threw up his hands in disgust. *Why did Mattie have to show up now?*

***

Darcie tried to keep her knees from quaking as she watched Mattie slowly descend the stairs of the hotel. The woman knew she had an audience downstairs and she played it to her advantage.

Mattie had changed her dress since Darcie saw her at the ranch. This robin's egg blue silk dress had enough yards of material to outfit a family of girls. Instead of a full crinoline to make her waist smaller, she wore the newest fashion of a bustle. Neither style of skirt fullness was practical in this frontier town, but Darcie still felt a pang of jealously. Not only because of her own plain cotton dress, but because this was the woman Reuben had loved and had a child with. How could Darcie compete with her looks and wealth when Reuben came to his senses and went back East with his family?

"Well, I hope these kind law officers are here to protect me from your rude behavior, Reuben," Mattie said as she flicked her eyes around the room of people.

Adam stepped forward with authority written all over his stiff posture. "I'm Marshal Wilerson, and this is my deputy, Ennis Donovan, a former *Chicago* police detective," Adam addressed Mattie. "Donovan is also the father of my wife Millie and her sister Darcie Robbins, who you already met at the Bar E Ranch."

"Also with us is Lyle Elison, a *Boston* lawyer who recently moved to Kansas to be near his sister's family. Mr. Elison handled the adoption of Tate and Amelia Robbins for Mr. Shepard."

"You adopted two children?" Mattie quickly asked as a second of panic crossed her face.

"Yes," Reuben sternly replied. "I am legally responsible for two children, no matter where I live, or to whom I am—or am not—married.

"But because of your accusations of our marriage status, I've asked Messrs. Elison, Wilerson and Donovan to investigate your claim that we're still married," Reuben bluntly stated.

"There is no need to do that. *I said* we're still married and we need to head back to New York immediately." Mattie's lips thinned showing her displeasure with Reuben's lack of belief in her.

"I'm staying here, working and taking care of my charges while Mr. Elison finds out the truth about our marriage. He's already written to Mr. Abercrombie, your late husband's lawyer, about Gabe's inheritance. It's just a matter of time before it's straightened out."

"And what if your local committee doesn't find out anything different?"

"I'll travel back to Rochester with you in two weeks to sort this out face to face with Mr. Abercrombie," Rueben challenged her

"It could take longer than two weeks to get this done, Reuben," Lyle sternly warned him.

"Two weeks, Mattie. And in the meantime, I want Gabe and Mary to spend time together, without interference."

"You have no right to…"

"I want to see Gabe, Mother. Please?" A slender girl slowly descended down the stairs toward the lobby. Apparently, she had been hiding at the top of the stairs listening in on the conversation below her. Her light brown hair, matching her mother's coloring, was spun in ringlets draping down her back. Her lavender dress probably cost more than a year's worth of groceries for Darcie's children.

"Mary, I told you…"

Adam stepped forward. "Nice to meet you, Miss Ringwald. I saw you arrive in town this morning with your mother. I'm sure Gabe will be happy to see you."

Mattie's eyes narrowed as she looked at the ring of people surrounding Reuben, then stopped a second to look at Darcie.

"Very well, then. I'm sure my children will be happy to reunite, and look forward to going home with us in two weeks, Reuben. In the meantime, I request you spend time with me, *your wife*, rather than with the local maid, even if you have adopted her fatherless offspring."

Darcie felt her face redden with embarrassment. How could she get through the next two weeks with everyone in town knowing she had been spending time with a married man?

"Bring Gabe into town this evening and we can all dine in the hotel here at six o–clock. Looks like that's the best place in this little town to eat. And be sure Gabe wears better clothes than what I saw him in today. He looked like a dirty immigrant."

Mattie turned, gathered her skirt and climbed the steps, pulling her daughter along when she got to the step where the child had rooted during the conversation.

Darcie prayed this matter with Mattie was resolved quickly or else...*what?* What if Reuben was still married to Mattie? Why had Darcie fallen in love with him, and let her children call him Poppa?

CHAPTER 11

"Reuben! Stop! Don't get on the train! I just received a letter from Mr. Abercrombie!"

Reuben whirled around at Lyle's shout. Would the letter reveal Mattie's conviction that they were still married, or something else?

The last two weeks had been hard on him, Darcie and all their children. For some strange reason, records of Mattie and Reginald's ceremony seemed to have vanished from the courthouse, or someone had been paid not to reveal them. Only Reuben and Mattie's ceremony was on record.

Darcie and her children stayed secluded in the ranch house, not even going into town for church. A couple of times Reuben saw Tate sitting on the porch sucking on his thumb and petting Yipper. But as soon as Tate saw Reuben, he'd run into the house instead of running to greet Reuben like he used to do. It hurt so bad that Tate had lost his love and trust for him.

Meanwhile, Reuben had to spend time with Mattie, so Gabe and Mary could see each other. He and Gabe had rode into town almost every evening after work and met Mattie and Mary for their evening meal.

"Rueben, let's get on the train. That letter will just state venomous lies. Mr. Abercrombie never liked me," Mattie pulled on his arm, trying to get him to follow her.

Gabe squeezed past his mother and jumped off the car steps. "I'm not going anywhere until I hear what he says since you never gave me my letter from Father...uh, Reginald," Gabe accused his mother while moving to stand by Lyle.

Reuben pulled Mattie's gripped hand off of his and backed down the steps. "I've been waiting for answers for two weeks. Hopefully, this letter will clear me of our marriage."

"But the train is ready to leave!" Mattie panicked, probably not at the fact that the train was leaving, but that the truth was going to be revealed, and she didn't want him to know it.

"We have fifteen minutes before the train is scheduled to leave. Mary, would you like to join your brother while we wait for the letter to be read?" Reuben asked calmly. Something was going on with Mattie and he didn't want the girl to get caught in the middle of trouble. Reuben grabbed Mattie's hand and pulled her out of the way so Mary could descend the steps. Gabe held out his hand and his sister went to grip it and lean against him.

Reuben looked to Darcie, standing by her family and friends, her face wet with tears, clutching Amelia tightly to her chest. They had come to the depot to tell him and Gabe good–bye. Tate's face was turned into the hollow of his Aunt Millie's neck, not wanting to look at anyone.

"Lyle, would you read the letter to us?" Reuben stated calmly, but inside, his heart was pounding like he was running up the side of a mountain. Everyone watched as Lyle slid his finger under the seal of the envelope flap and started to take out the piece of paper.

"NO!" Mattie screeched, lunging for the letter in Lyle's hand. Lyle was caught off guard at her attack and dropped the still folded letter and envelope to the ground. Mattie dropped to the ground to retrieve it, but Adam's booted foot stomped on the letter, just as she started to pick it up. She tried twisting the letter out from under his boot, but only achieved to tearing off a corner of the paper.

"You're obstructing justice, Mrs. Ringwald. I can escort you to the jailhouse if you prefer not to cooperate in the reading of this letter."

Mattie's shocked face turned up to the marshal said it all. She hadn't been telling the truth about something, and didn't want Reuben to know what it was.

Adam lifted Mattie up on her feet and set her aside before retrieving the letter under his boot. He placed a hand around her forearm to keep hold of her while he handed the letter back to Lyle.

Lyle looked at Reuben. "Are you sure you want this read out loud in public? I suggest we move over to my office to hear the contents."

"You can't read the letter now! We need to get on the train before it leaves," Mattie squeaked.

Dagmar strolled over to Lyle. "I'll go get their trunks off the train. They can always take a later train if they are still going to New York." He lightly squeezed Gabe's shoulder in support before he left.

"All right, let's go to your office. It's just down the street," Reuben motioned to Lyle.

As Reuben started walking down the street, he realized Darcie was quickly walking in the other direction. "Darcie," he called out while jogging to her side and putting his hand on her shoulder to stop her. "I want you to hear what the letter says. The way Mattie is acting, I'm assuming it's a good thing for us." It hurt seeing Darcie look so miserable and resigned to their separation. He wrapped his arms around her and Amelia to convey his need. "Please, Darcie," he whispered in her ear. "I love you and I *will* make the five of us a family. I might have to go to Rochester to clear this up, but I will get a divorce from Mattie so we can marry. She hasn't been my wife for years, and she's never going to be so again."

"I'm scared I'm losing you, Reuben." Darcie's fresh tears soaked through his shirt, causing him to hold her more tightly. Then she pulled back to look at his face. "But I want you to do what's right for Gabe. He comes first."

All Reuben could do was shake his head to confirm her statement, because as parents, they both agreed their children came first.

"Please come in with me to Lyle's office, Darcie. I'll still need your support as a friend if everything goes haywire with the reading of this letter," he pleaded and sought her eyes for her agreement.

Darcie sighed and walked back to her family. "Flora, will you take Amelia for me? I'm going with Rueben." Darcie handed her daughter over, then took Reuben's hand. "Okay, let's hear what the attorney has to say." Then she hesitated and asked, "Do you want Gabe and Mary to hear the letter, too?"

"Lyle," Reuben called out to get his attention. "Can you quickly scan the letter to see if the children should hear the contents, too?"

Mattie miss stepped and would have crumpled to the ground if Adam hadn't had a hold of her arm. "Please don't let them hear it. They'll hate me," she wailed.

Lyle was silent for a few moments while he read through the letter. "It states his wishes for both children, and explains why. I think the children have a right to hear it—if they want to do so. If not, I'll take care of Ringwald's instructions through Mr. Abercrombie," Lyle answered Reuben, ignoring Mattie.

"Gabe and Mary, it's up to you," Reuben said looking at one, then the other. "And if either one of you don't want to hear it, that's fine," Reuben suggested.

"I want to hear it," Gabe clearly stated. He squeezed his sister's hand and said to her. "If you don't want to, I'll tell you the main part of the letter later."

The girl's face was red, looking ready to cry, poor thing. What would the letter reveal about her parents?

"Fine. Let them hear what the lawyer had to say. Maybe they'll learn a few things about Reginald they should know," Mattie huffed.

"Mary? It's your choice," Lyle softly said to the girl.

She looked down, not meeting Lyle's eyes but nodding, indicating she wanted to stay.

Lyle led the way to his office, stopping to unlock the door before they could enter. "I just went down to the post office to mail some letters, and found the letter from Abercrombie. I'm so glad I got it before you left, Reuben," Lyle shook his head, probably glad he could help his client. "I don't have enough chairs for everyone in the front room, so I guess three of you can sit down if you want and the rest will have to stand. He waited for someone to take a seat, but all parties remained standing.

"All right, I'll read the letter now," Lyly cleared his throat and read out loud.

"Mr. Elison, please pass this letter onto Mr. Reuben Shepard."

"Dear Mr. Shepard,

I'm sorry I wasn't available when you visited my office about Reginald Ringwald's letter to Gabriel. As Reginald's lawyer and friend, I want to explain his wishes to you.

To state it bluntly, he thought you had died in the war, and he married Matilda at her request. Reginald was shocked when you arrived home after the war, then knowing what Matilda and her parents had done to ensure his marriage to her. He realized she had married him for his money, not for her love of him.

Reginald started two accounts in the Rochester Bank after your visit in 1865.

One bank account is for you. Mr. Shepard, and Reginald faithfully added what would have been your war pension, plus fifty percent of the income Matilda received on her marriage to you from her parents."

"Half of...? *What?!* He'll get five thousand dollars?! I'll contest that in court!" Mattie fumed.

"Please be quiet, Mrs. Ringwald, so Mr. Elison can continue," Adam warned her.

Five thousand dollars? Did she just say...five thousand dollars?! Reuben felt the room start to spin until Darcie squeezed his hand to make him focus on Lyle.

"Thank you, Adam. To continue…

"Gabriel was listed as the beneficiary in case of your death. Reginald hoped you would eventually return so he could give the money, and an apology, directly to you.

"The other bank account is in Gabriel's name, with you, Mr. Shepard, as the beneficiary if something would happen to Gabriel. Reginald put twenty–five percent of the income Matilda received on her marriage to you in Gabriel's account, which, as yours, has been drawing interest since 1865."

Lyle paused to look at Mattie, then continued.

"Reginald's will states the money in his bank account will be split three ways. One third each to Matilda, Mary and Gabriel. The children's money is in a trust and available when they turn eighteen. And Gabriel is Mary's benefactor, not Matilda. The bulk of Reginald's estate, excluding the house Matilda lives in, goes to his two brothers.

"To be sure Gabriel received his letter, which revealed your name and your bank account information, Reginald stated in a letter directly to Matilda, that if she interfered and Gabriel did not get his letter within a month of Reginald's death, she lost her split of the money and the house, which

Reginald had bought from her father. The house would be sold and the income would be split between his two brothers. Gabriel's letter instructed him to come to my office to show me Reginald's hand–written letter, then Reginald's bank account would be divided three ways according to his wishes.

"In researching to be sure he was indeed married to Matilda, Reginald found out a judge had been paid to declare you, Mr. Shepard, dead, and to annul your marriage, even though Gabriel was proof that your marriage had been consummated.

"Looking into the matter now myself, I found that Matilda's marriage to Reginald had also been erased a few days after Reginald's death, but this time the person has been caught.

"I pray Matilda will do the right thing and give Gabriel his letter by the time this letter reaches you. Gabriel will not have to come back to show me the letter if he can identify the special mark only he and Reginald shared which was hidden in the letter. If Gabriel has not received the letter by a month of Reginald's death, please telegraph me right away so I can proceed with Reginald's wishes.

"Sincerely yours,

"Robert Abercrombie, Attorney"

The room was quiet, everyone shocked at what the letter said.

Reuben stared at Mattie when Lyle finished reading the letter. But Mattie looked defiantly back at Reuben, looking as though she hated him with all her being. She *knew* what Reginald's will said, but kept the letter away from Gabe anyway. *And why?* If Reuben had renewed his vows with Mattie within the month of Reginald's death, did she think she'd control everyone's money? Reuben bet that was her scheme all along when coming to Kansas so soon after her husband died. *How could I have been so stupid?! I fell for her act twice!*

Reuben hated to look at Darcie, worried she'd think him stupid, too. When he did, she wasn't paying any attention to him, but standing with Gabe and Mary instead. Mary's face was crushed into Gabe's chest, and her brother was rubbing her back to comfort her. And Darcie was slowly rubbing Gabe's back. Darcie was a good mother and automatically worrying how the letter affected the children. Darcie was such a contrast from the children's scheming mother.

Then it dawned on him. *He wasn't married to Mattie after all.* He was free to do what he wanted. The nightmare of his past lifted off his shoulders.

Lyle cleared his throat to get everyone's attention, "Mrs. Ringwald, do I answer back that Gabriel has received his letter, or do I tell Mr. Abercrombie to split Mr. Ringwald's bank account in half instead of thirds *and* put your house up for sale?"

If looks could kill, the town's undertaker would be busy this afternoon. Mattie was fuming mad, not embarrassed for being caught trying to steal the money her husband had given to others. Fortunately, Reginald didn't trust his own wife, and Mattie was now paying for it.

Mattie looked at the door, and Adam stepped in front of it. It didn't matter if she did get out the door and try to run, Reuben would physically tackle her on the boardwalk, he was so mad at what she had put their son through.

"Mrs. Ringwald? Do you have the letter in question? I advise you to hand it to Gabriel if you do," Adam put in his two cents' worth now.

She didn't answer verbally but pulled open the strings of her reticule. Mattie pulled out a folded envelope and thrust it at Gabe. "Here. Look it over and see if you find your secret mark you two had," she hissed.

Gabe took it, seeing the envelope had been opened. "You read my letter, Mother."

"I had to see what my *dear* husband said to you." She folded her arms, waiting for proof it was indeed Reginald's letter.

After a minute of silence, Lyle asked, "Is this the original letter from Mr. Ringwald, or has it been forged?"

Gabe had a faint smile on his lips. "It's real."

"So what's the mark to tell it is so?" Mattie questioned.

"I'll never tell, Mother." Gabe walked to Lyle's desk. "Here's the letter, Mr. Elison. Now you can get back to Mr. Abercrombie."

"Thank you, Gabe," Lyle shifted papers on his desk. "There is one more thing which must be decided before anyone travels back to New York."

Reuben held his breath. What would Mattie say to his request? And would Darcie still want to marry him and adopt Gabe?

"Mrs. Ringwald, Mr. Shepard had asked that you sign over your parental rights to Gabriel Shepard, to him. Do you so agree? You would then have no contact with your son unless you had permission from Mr. Shepard until Gabriel is eighteen. After which time, Gabriel is an adult and makes his own decisions."

"Still planning on marrying your little Irish maid and having her be Gabe's new momma, Reuben?" Mattie asked sweetly, but with a hint of irritation.

"This request has nothing to do with any future plans between Mrs. Robbins and myself. It is to protect Gabe from you, as long as Gabe wants it in place."

"Get out your pen and bottle of ink, Mr. Elison, because I'll gladly sign to get rid of Gabe. He looks too much like Reuben."

The gasps in the room made Mattie smile instead of cringe. Reuben looked at Gabe to see his narrowed eyes staring at his mother. This moment would haunt his son forever, but hopefully, he was old enough to understand this was his mother's lack of compassion, not about his worth.

"I want Mary to stay with me, Mother. I'm in charge of her affairs now," Gabe defiantly stated, not realizing it wasn't quite as easy as he proposed. Mary still had one living parent, and the girl was only twelve years old.

Mattie turned to her children hand on her hip, eyeing them like they were two stray dogs. "Well Mary, do you want to stay in this *backward* frontier town with all these *immigrants*, or return to New York with me? I really don't care."

"How can you say that to your daughter?!" Darcie asked incredulously. She moved to stand in front of Gabe and Mary as if to protect them.

"Because I *don't* care. In fact, it might be easier for me to marry a wealthy man if I don't have her underfoot. Maybe I'll send her to live with one of Reginald's brothers since they inherited all the money I should have gotten," Mattie retorted.

"Sign over your parental rights to Mary to me then, *right now.* I would love to have Mary as my daughter. You go back to your life in New York, free to do whatever you please." Darcie's face was red from anger and her eyes narrowed with determination.

"Huh. Really?" Mattie put a finger on her screwed up mouth, pretending to seriously think about it. *Would she really give up her daughter?*

Gabe pulled Mary from his chest to look in her face. "Please say you want to stay with me, Mary. Would you want to live with Mother without me there to protect you?"

"Protect her? You think I'm some kind of monster?!" Mattie's hands were on her hips now as she leaned toward Darcie and the children. Mattie looked around the room when no one spoke a word.

"*Fine.* Mr. Elison, fill out the papers I need to sign her over to her new mother. I'm going over to the depot to change my ticket to the next train, *and* throw their things out of my luggage. I'll be back to sign the papers before I leave," Mattie pushed past Adam, yanked open the door and stormed out of Lyle's office.

Was Mattie this mean to her children all the time? Why didn't he get Gabe out of that household sooner? Reuben questioned himself.

Darcie had pulled Mary over to the chairs, and they sat together, Darcie hugging and murmuring words he couldn't hear. Mary clung to Darcie, sobbing from the hurt and confusion her mother had dealt her.

Gabe stood next to them, keeping a hand on Mary's shaking shoulder.

"Should I go ahead and fill out the papers, or will Mattie come back apologizing, wanting Mary to return home with her?" Lyle looked between Reuben and Adam, confused at the woman's outburst and what to do because of it.

Gabe looked at Reuben a minute then turned to Mary. "Sis, Clear Creek is about as opposite a place to Rochester as you can get, and it was kind of hard to adjust at first. But now in only a short time, I have friends, honorary grandparents, aunts and uncles who really care about me. Tate and Amelia love me as a big brother...and... Darcie would be ten times a better parent than our mother ever was. Please stay here with me," Gabe pleaded on his final request.

Mary pulled out of Darcie's arms to stare at her brother, then Reuben and finally at Darcie's smiling but tear-stained face. "Do you really want me?" Mary's whispered words to Darcie about cracked his heart.

"Oh child, I'd *love* to have you as my daughter. I already love your brother and he loves me... most of the time." Darcie nudged Gabe's shoulder, reminding him of the good and bad times they'd had to this point. "There will be some trying times as we adjust to become a family, but it will be so worth it.

"Reuben?" Darcie pulled him into the conversation. "Do you want to add anything to convince Mary to become part of our family?" All three of them looked up at him. Here was his chance to make things right for Gabe, Darcie and him.

He got down on his knees in front of Mary and gently took her little hands. "Sweetheart, I promise I will love and protect you always, just as I will do for your brother, Darcie, Tate and Amelia. It sounds like your father was a good man, and you need to keep the good memories of those years in your heart. But, sadly, he's gone now. Darcie and I would be honored if you'd be our daughter, Mary Shepard." Reuben wasn't going to bring up the possibility she really could be his daughter. He'd have Lyle check her birth records first, and decide what to do after that.

Mary took a deep breath before answering, "Okay, I want to stay."

"How soon can we become a family?" Gabe looked puzzled now, realizing there was work involved besides signing some papers.

While Reuben was wrestling with the same thought, Darcie spoke up. "Recently some of our extended family, Sarah and Marcus Brenner, adopted eight orphaned children. Besides conducting a marriage ceremony for the couple, Pastor Reagan had a kind of ceremony to bless the new family.

"Reuben, could you see when Pastor Reagan can do a wedding and family ceremony for our family, too?" He couldn't help grinning. Darcie was accepting his proposal!

"We need a house first. We can't all fit in Pa's bunk room", Gabe added, thinking how small the room was with the two of them in it.

Reuben reached for Darcie's hand while Gabe started plotting their future. It was finally going to happen! And he had a lot to do to get ready.

"So where would we live? Would it be on the ranch?" Gabe turned from talking to him to Mary instead. "Just wait 'til you see the Bar E Ranch, Mary. There's dogs and cats, chickens, horses and more cows that you can count.

"I know how to ride a horse and help with the cattle drives. The ranch horses are named for the Galaxy and I like to ride Saturn or Leo. Uncle Dag's horse is Comet and Aunt Cora's is Moon. I'd like to ride Dipper one day, but he's still a bucking horse so I have to get better at bustin' broncs first."

"Uh, it'll be a while before you're ready to ride Dipper, or Snot," Reuben chuckled, looking at Mary's reactions to the horses' names. At least she had quit crying now.

"Maybe we should live in town. Instead of being a drover, maybe I'd open a shop in Clear Creek." Thanks to the money Reginald set aside for Reuben, he could plan for the future of their combined family.

"And I believe we need to conduct a family meeting for everyone's input before we make our decisions of where to live and what we do. Don't you agree, *Poppa* Reuben?" Darcie wisely injected to tease him.

"Yep, and Tate and Amelia need to be in on the conversation, too."

"Why? They can't really talk yet," Gabe questioned Reuben.

"Because they are part of our family, isn't that right, *Momma* Darcie?"

EPILOGUE

Mid November

"Read, Sissie." Darcie, standing by the wood stove, glanced over her shoulder at Tate as he trailed behind Mary, who had just arrived home from school.

"Just a second, Tate. I need to put down my school work and take off my coat." Tate held the book over his head while jumping up and down beside her. "What book are we reading *again* today?"

Darcie smiled wondering how many times they had all read Tate's favorite book to him in the last month.

"Ma," Gabe called, as he breezed through the door and set his school lunch pail and books on the side table. "Some of us are going over to help Lyle set up the furniture."

"Wait, I…" Gabe was trotting back to the kitchen door as she tried to talk to him.

"I got to go! Angus and Fergus are already there!"

"Come back here!" Darcie yelled at him.

"What?" Gabe had his hand on the door handle and ready to run out of hearing distance.

"I made molasses cookies for you to bring over for your friends," Darcie called out.

That brought him running back to the kitchen to grab the tin she held out to him. Gabe's grin warmed her heart. "Thanks, Ma!" And he took off for the door again.

Lyle had a carpenter turn the big room in the back of his lawyer's office into an apartment, consisting of a bedroom, washroom, kitchen and living area. Furniture ordered for the apartment came in on the train today, and was sitting on the depot dock ready to move. Lyle had offered money to a few boys to move everything to his building and into place.

So many things had changed in the last six weeks for the combined Shepard family. They rented a two–story wooden home in Clear Creek, a block away from Millie and Adam's house, and moved in after their family wedding ceremony.

After Reuben's money from Mr. Reginald had transferred to their local bank, Reuben opened the Shepard and Sons Saddle Shop next to the livery. Even though Gabe and Tate weren't old enough to help run the business, Reuben was proud to acknowledge them in his business name. So far, most of Reuben's business was repairing harnesses and all sorts of horse tack, but his goal was to build custom–made saddles.

Gabe had adjusted well to the move to Clear Creek, probably more so because Reuben was his father, and he was older. He'd grown at least three inches and added fifteen pounds since he first came to Kansas.

Mary still mourned the loss of her father and talked about him, but rarely her mother. The act of being left behind when Mattie left was devastating to the child. After checking dates and facts, Mary was more likely to be Reginald's daughter not Reuben's, but it didn't matter. Both Reuben and Darcie was listed as her parents now.

Darcie and Reuben were supporting Mary during her grieving but it was "Grandma Flora" who had helped the girl the most. Flora invited her over to spend Saturday afternoons with her, baking something special for the boarders and for Mary to bring home to her new family.

Tate and Amelia loved their new siblings, but like all kids, they fought at times. To go from them having all of her attention, to have to share her with three other people was a challenge. Especially since Tate and Amelia were sharing a room, him sleeping in a trundle bed and Amelia in a crib. Darcie and Reuben decided in the beginning of their marriage they weren't going to have the children sleeping with them unless they needed comforting. They wanted privacy to bond their marriage. And their house was big enough to give Gabe and Mary their own rooms, too.

Darcie sensed someone looking at her and turned to see Reuben leaning against the kitchen doorframe, watching the domestic scene in the kitchen. He must have come into the house when Gabe raced out. Reuben hadn't taken off his hat and coat, so apparently he was just stopping in for a minute.

"You're home early. Everything okay at the shop?"

"Yes, everything's fine. I promised a lovely young lady," Reuben walked over to Mary and gently put his hands on her shoulders, "that I'd take her somewhere special today and we need to be there in ten minutes."

This was news to Darcie, but it didn't matter she hadn't been told. Reuben was working hard at making Mary feel included in the family.

"Where are we going?" Mary asked hesitantly.

"A place all women love."

Mary didn't say anything as she looked between Darcie and Reuben. All Darcie could do was shrug her shoulders because she didn't know anything about Reuben's surprise. "It's a surprise to me too, Mary."

"I saw a really pretty dark green velvet fabric in Taylor's Mercantile back a while," Reuben hinted. He grinned when he could see it dawned on Mary it was the velvet she'd looked at more than once while in the store. Her eyes grew wide with excitement.

"Mary, we have an appointment at the dress shop. Mrs. Ressig is going to make you a dress to wear for the church's

Christmas pageant. I told her you liked the green velvet in the mercantile, but *you* get to decide what fabric and trim you want."

"Really?" Mary squealed with excitement. "I get a new dress?"

Darcie was sure Mattie had always dressed Mary to flaunt the family's wealth and social status. But the idea of Reuben doing something special for the girl, even if it was just another dress, made Mary beam.

"Yes, you do, if you're okay with it," Reuben added. He was so good with all four children, a confident father figure they all needed.

"Oh course I am! I'll get my coat and be ready to go!"

"Read book!" Tate whined, looking distressed his reader was going to disappear out the door.

"Tate, how about you read your book to your little Sissie and me? I'm sure you know it now by heart, and we'd love to hear it."

"Okay!" He pushed a kitchen chair up next to the high chair where Amelia sat, and opened the book on the table in front of her. Tate still had his share of tantrums, but living with two parents and three siblings in a stable home had calmed his past fears.

"Poppa," Reuben's eyes caught Darcie's a second when hearing Mary call him by the endearment instead of her usual address of his first name.

"I'm right here, Mary," Reuben said, promising her more than being in the present for just the moment.

"Could my...little sister...have a new dress too?" Mary looked so hopeful to Reuben that Darcie had to shut her eyes to stop the tears from falling. Not only was Mary finally feeling comfortable with asking Reuben for something, but she was considering herself part of their combined family.

"That's a wonderful suggestion, Honey. How about we bundle up Amelia and take her with us? You can choose her fabric and trim, too."

Mary turned to Darcie, with concern in her eyes. "Is that all right, Momma?" Darcie walked over to her adopted daughter and pulled her into her arms, then gave her a kiss on top of the head.

"That's a great suggestion, Mary. Amelia—and Tate—are so lucky to have you as their big sister." Darcie quickly wiped her eyes with one hand before pulling away from Mary so she could look into Mary's eyes. "Your poppa and I are so proud of you."

Mary wrapped her arms around Darcie's middle, and she barely heard Mary's "Thank you, Momma."

Darcie looked up as Reuben put his arm around her shoulders. "I think we have us a fine family, don't you think, *Momma* Darcie?" Reuben gave her a quick, but tender kiss on her lips.

"I sure do believe so, *Poppa* Reuben." Darcie said, while trying not to let her tears choke her words.

She and Reuben had survived bad marriages, but now their love made a rock solid family for four children and a loving marriage for themselves. She never thought running away to a frontier cattle town would solve her problems, but this is where she found love with a Kansas drover.

The End

Brides with Grit Series

I hope you enjoyed reading *Darcie Desires a Drover*. Please help other readers discover my books by recommending them to family and friends, either by word of mouth or writing a review. I'd really appreciate it.

The series setting is based on the famous old cowtown of Ellsworth, Kansas during its cattle drive days. The town of Clear Creek though, is fictional, based on the many little towns that sprang up as the railroad was built across Kansas.

This particular area is now the current Kanopolis State Park in central Kansas. Being local to where I live, I've hiked the park's hiking trails, where it's easy to visualize what the area looked like in 1873—because it remains the same now—as then.

Although not all of the **Brides with Grit** titles may be published as of this book's printing, please visit **www.LindaHubalek.com** or ask your favorite retailer or library to find out when they will be available. You don't have to, but I recommend reading the books in order to get full benefit of the story line.

Rania Ropes a Rancher (Rania and Jacob)

Millie Marries a Marshal (Millie and Adam)

Hilda Hogties a Horseman (Hilda and Noah)

Cora Captures a Cowboy (Cora and Dagmar)

Sarah Snares a Soldier (Sarah and Marcus)

Cate Corrals a Cattleman (Cate and Isaac)

Darcie Desires a Drover (Darcie and Reuben)

Tina Tracks a Trail Boss (Tina and Leif)

Also read <u>*Lilly: Bride of Illinois*</u>, a spin-off book in the *American Mail-Order Brides Series.*

Historical Fiction Books by Linda K. Hubalek

Trail of Thread Series

Find out what it was like for the thousands of families who made the cross-country journey into the unknown. "Stitch" your way across country with these letters and quilt diagrams from the 1800s. This series feature history from 1854 to 1865.

Trail of Thread Series, Book 1

Taste the dust of the road and feel the wind in your face as you travel with a Kentucky family by wagon train to the new territory of Kansas in 1854.

Trail of Thread Series, Book 2

Experience the terror of the fighting and the determination to endure as you stake a claim alongside the women caught in the bloody conflicts of Kansas in the 1850's.

Trail of Thread Series, Book 3

Feel the uncertainty, doubt, and danger faced by the pioneer women as they defend their homes and pray for their men during the Civil War.

Tying the Knot: Kansas Quilter Series, Book 1 continues the family saga into the next generations.

Butter in the Well Series

This historical fiction series is based on the actual Swedish family who homesteaded the author's childhood home.

Butter in the Well, Book 1

Read the fictionalized account of Kajsa Svenson Runeberg, an emigrant wife who recounts, through her diary, how she and her family built up a farm on the unsettled Kansas prairie from 1868 to 1888.

Prairie Bloomin, Book 2 '

Prairie Bloomin' features the 1889 to 1900 diary of daughter Alma Swenson, as she grows up on the farm her parents homesteaded.

Egg Gravy, Book 3

Faded recipes. We've all come across them from time to time in our lives, either handwritten by ourselves or by another person in our family, or as old yellowed newspaper clippings stuck in a cookbook of sorts.

Looking Back, Book 4

Kajsa Svensson Runeberg, now age seventy-five, looks back at the changes she has experienced on the farm she homesteaded fifty-one years ago. She reminisces about the past, resolves the present situation, and looks toward their future off the farm.

Planting Dreams Series

Can you imagine starting a journey to an unknown country in 1868, not knowing what the country would be like, where you would live, or how you would survive? Did you make the right decision to leave in the first place?

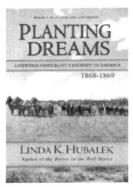  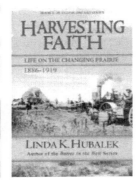

Planting Dreams, Book 1

This first book in the *Planting Dreams* series portrays Swedish immigrant Charlotta Johnson (author Linda Hubalek's ancestor), as she ponders the decision to leave her homeland, travel to America, and worries about her family's future in a new country.

Cultivating Hope, Book 2

This family faced countless challenges as they homestead on America's Great Plains during the 1800s. Years of hard work develop the land and improve the quality of life for her family—but not with a price.

Harvesting Faith, Book 3

Imagine surveying your farmstead on the last day of your life, reviewing the decades of joys, hardships, and changes that have taken place on the eighty acres you have called home for the past fifty years. Would you feel at peace or find remorse at the decisions that took place in your life?

About the Author

Linda Hubalek grew up on the Kansas prairie, always wanting to be a farmer like her parents and ancestors. After earning a college degree in Agriculture, marriage took Linda away from Kansas as her husband worked in engineering jobs in several states.

Meanwhile, Linda wrote books about pioneer women who homesteaded in Kansas between 1854 to the early 1900s, especially her Swedish immigrant ancestors.

Linda Hubalek and her husband eventually moved back home to Kansas, where they raised American buffalo (bison) for a dozen years.

Linda is currently writing sweet wholesome historical romance series set in the 1800s.

Linda loves to connect with her readers, so please contact her through one of these social media sites.

www.LindaHubalek.com

www.Twitter.com/LindaHubalek

www.Facebook.com/LindaHubalekbooks

www.Pinterest.com/LindaHubalek

Please sign up for her newsletter at **www.LindaHubalek.com** to hear about the release of future books, contests and more.

If you enjoyed her books, please post reviews on your favorite book sites. Thank you!

Order to: Butterfield Books Inc., PO Box 407, Lindsborg KS 67456

Orders: **1-785-227-9250**   Email: **staff@ButterfieldBooks.com**

Order online at www.ButterfieldBooks.com

Send to:

Name _____

Address _____

Town, St_____ Zip _____

☐ **Check** enclosed, payable to **Butterfield Books Inc.**

☐ **Charge my credit card**

Card # _____Exp_____CVV _____

Signature _____

Romance Titles	Qty	Unit Price	Total
Rania Ropes a Rancher		11.95	
Millie Marries a Marshal		11.95	
Hilda Hogties a Horseman		11.95	
Cora Captures a Cowboy		11.95	
Sarah Snares a Soldier		11.95	
Cate Corrals a Cattleman		11.95	
Darcie Desires a Drover		11.95	
Lilly: Bride of Illinois		11.95	
S/H per address: $3.00 for 1st book, Each add'tl $.50			
Ship into KS? Add 9.50% tax			
Total			

129

Order to: Butterfield Books Inc., PO Box 407, Lindsborg KS 67456

Orders: **1-785-227-9250**   Email: **staff@ButterfieldBooks.com**

Order online at www.ButterfieldBooks.com

Send to:

Name _____

Address _____

Town, St_____ Zip _____

☐ **Check** enclosed, payable to **Butterfield Books Inc.**

☐ **Charge my credit card**

Card # _____Exp_____CVV _____

Signature _____

Historical Fiction Titles	Qty	Unit Price	Total
Butter in the Well		11.95	
Prairie Bloomin'		11.95	
Egg Gravy		11.95	
Looking Back		11.95	
Butter Series (all 4 books)		**42.95**	
Trail of Thread		11.95	
Thimble of Soil		11.95	
Stitch of Courage		11.95	
Trail Series (all 3 books)		**32.95**	
Planting Dreams		11.95	
Cultivating Hope		11.95	
Harvesting Faith		11.95	
Planting Series (all 3 books)		**32.95**	
Tying the Knot		11.95	
S/H per address: $3.00 for 1st book, Each add'tl $.50			
Ship into KS? Add 9.50% tax			
Total			

Made in the USA
Middletown, DE
27 March 2016